The Last Witch

Beyond The Veil 3.5

M J Lawrie

Copyright

Chapter 1

I could watch her sleep for the rest of my life. Watch her wake. Watch her eat. Watch her play and tantrum. I'd even take watching her cry as long as I can see her. As long as she is safe.

My dearest Callie. My sweet daughter.

I reach out and sweep the dark brown mess of curly hair from her beautiful little face. Her eyes dance behind her lids as I rest my hand on her cheek and close my eyes.

I see her dreams. They're of me. Of us today. In her dreams, we sit in the meadow behind our home and watch a fawn graze alongside his mother. Dream-Callie and dream-me hide in the long grass, watching in silence as the cute little thing stumbles on his new, long, uncoordinated legs.

Callie sits in my lap and twirls my hair in her dainty little fingers before she loses interest, and we make daisy chains and chase butterflies instead.

It's a beautiful dream. The dream of a young and untainted heart. And that is what she is.

Young and untainted by the cruelty and blood-soaked world I saved us all from.

It's been six months since I arrived back in the Arcane Realm.

Six glorious months.

I continue to stand in the meadow, watching dream-Lilly and dream-Callie create endless daisy chains. I remain alone in the dream, but the hand I feel on my shoulder tells me I'm not alone in the real world.

'What is she dreaming about?' he asks before planting a warm kiss on my cheek.

'Come in here and see,' I whisper back, reaching out and taking his hand to place upon her head. In a swirl of smoke, another joins my side, standing in the meadow to watch the dream before us both. 'Isn't she just perfect?' I admire.

'Yes,' Gabriel replies with a soft smile. When I look at him, his brilliant blue eyes are on me. 'She takes after her most perfect mother.'

He plants another kiss on my knuckles before turning to watch her. His fingers entwine with mine, and we stand side by side, silent and lost in the simple dreams of a happy child.

Gabriel's thumb traces back and forth over my knuckles in both the real world and this one. I smell his scent. Feel the warmth of his skin. The ebb of his patience and understanding as I keep him here with me for another night.

Sleep refuses to come easily for me. It always has, I guess. Being in a different realm has changed so much for me. For us all. There is no more war. No more hiding or running. No more humans.

But it seems the nightmares will never end for me.

'Daddy!' dream-Callie calls joyfully as dream-Gabriel strides towards the pair with a picnic basket in his hand. The same one we forgot before he rushed off to fetch it earlier today.

Her call startles the mother deer and her baby, and the two dart off into the trees.

Callie runs to Gabriel and leaps into his waiting arms.

I hold the same smile now as I do in the dream, watching the two most precious people in my life make their way towards the dream version of myself.

'And what have my girls been doing whilst I was away?' dream-Gabriel asks, sitting in the grass by my side.

Callie answers his question by sliding one of the enormous daisy chain necklaces we made over his head.

'I have been dreaming of spending our days like this for years,' Gabriel whispers beside me, his eyes glued to us all. 'It's almost as wonderful watching it as an outsider as it is living it.'

His hand tightens in mine, keeping me close. Checking I'm still here.

'Come,' he whispers. 'Let's get back to bed.'

I nod and pull back from my connection to her mind.

The sunshine of her dreams fade into the darkness of her bedroom.

I'm still kneeling on the floor at her bedside, so close to her face that her soft breaths land on my skin. Above, an enchanted ceiling twinkles with stars, acting as a night light for her. Her kitten, Shadow, slumbers at her feet, purring incessantly.

And sat beside me with a look of concern, my Gabriel.

Our hands are still knotted together as he reaches over with his other hand to tuck my long red hair behind my ear.

'Do you want to talk about it?' he asks in a low whisper.

'What is there to talk about?' I ask, knowing precisely what he means.

'The crack in our bedroom ceiling, for a start. And the fact that I hate waking up to find you gone.' He pulls me closer, so his arms wrap around my middle, and he places me on his lap.

'It was just another nightmare,' I reply, sinking into his touch as he softly kisses my cheek. 'I didn't want to wake you up again, so I thought I'd just walk it off.' I look at him with worry. 'I didn't realise I caused any damage. I put a crack in the ceiling?'

'Just a little one. It will be easy enough to fix.'

'Shame my head isn't so easy to patch up.'

Callie gives a light giggle and shuffles beneath her blanket before stilling once more and returning to her dreams.

'I think I lose a year of my life every time I open my eyes and you're not beside me,' Gabriel says.

His heart thumps harder beneath his chest and his lips brush gently over my skin, causing goosebumps to ripple over every inch of me.

'What did you dream about, my love?'

'I dreamt that he had her,' I tell him, the terror I felt in my dreams stirring at my core. 'I dreamt that Theo took Callie.' I swallow a painfully dry swallow. 'I just had to see her. I had to know she was okay.'

Gabriel stills, and every muscle in his body goes rigid. Even his grip on me becomes uncomfortable and I inwardly scold myself for my idiotic and insensitive mistake.

'I'm sorry. I shouldn't have said anything. I shouldn't have said that name-'

As I go to sit up, knowing I've just poked at a wound still healing within him from the betrayal and brutality of the man he believed to be his father, he yanks me back down and holds me even closer.

'I told you,' he insists. 'You're not allowed to say sorry to me. The *"S"* word is off-limits.'

He lets out a heavy breath and turns his face towards Callie, and we both watch her.

'No one will ever get her. Those monsters are long gone and no one else alive would dare attempt to harm a single hair on her head.'

'She's the next Arcane,' I say mournfully, hating the enormous amount of responsibility and danger that will place her under. 'Someone will try. One day.'

She still has her dark brown hair for now. We all keep waiting for the day her magic awakens and turns it red, signalling the transformation into an Arcane Witch.

It terrifies us. Absofuckinglutely terrifies us.

So many people have tried to claim one of my kind for their own, and with the most sadistic methods anyone could possibly conceive of. And the trail of chaos, destruction, and death that we have all somehow survived, still clings to us every day, following us. Haunting us.

'Theodore Kendryk is dead,' Gabriel says firmly. 'His body, along with Grayson's, lies in the darkness of the caves back in the human world.' Gabriel states these facts with coldness and finality. 'They are far from us. And far from our daughter. That fucker Hendrix too. Dead. Gone. You made sure of that.'

'I wish my brain would get the memo. Every night I dream they're in this house, coming for her.'

'I'll go in there and give your mind a good talking to if you like.' He rests his forehead against mine. 'Then maybe you can do the same and explain to my head that every time you leave my sight doesn't mean I've lost you again.'

I lean in, my lips rest on his, and again, every inch of me tingles.

It's been six months since we stood atop that hill, Lois Quinn and I, and performed the spell that sent us over here together. Six months since I first breathed in the fresh, unpolluted air of the Arcane Realm. Six months since I saw a fucking dragon do a flyby in recognition of the return of the Arcane Witch.

Six months since I reunited with my family, after five years of hell, living on the run with Mama Quinn and avoiding the humans who still hunted us.

And that was after a lifetime of horror at the hands of a monstrous uncle, his vindictive wife and their sadistic piece of shit son.

And another lifetime of blood, betrayal, heartbreak and carnage at the hands of the Kendryk men. Gabriel excluded, of course.

I know that they're gone. I know that the monsters who fought to own me, my magic, my body and my bloodline are as far from us as can be.

Grayson is dead. Theodore is dead. And Toby Smith is buried deep inside Bias's mind.

But yet, the nightmares still come. The feeling of dread refuses to relent.

I fear for my daughter.

I fear for us all.

It was a month before Callie would agree to sleep in her own bed after I returned. She wanted her mummy, and my God, I wanted my daughter in my arms as much as fucking possible. She's happy enough in her room now, but I can't seem to let go as easy. More often than not, Callie wakes to me sleeping in her room and, by extension, Gabriel.

'We can sleep in here again tonight,' Gabriel concedes, shifting himself into a more comfortable position. His back leans against Callie's bed and his legs stretch out as he repositions me on his frame and yawns.

'You sure you don't mind?' I ask, still watching our daughter sleep and instantly relaxing at his words.

'I'll sleep on a bed of nails and it would still be heaven if I've got the pair of you in my sights.'

I snuggle down and close my eyes. The same as last night, the night before that and the one before that.

'I love you, Beautiful.'

'I love you more.'

He kisses me on the top of my head and closes his eyes. 'Impossible. That, my love, is simply impossible.'

Within a few minutes, Callie shifts in her bed. She sleepily slides out and crawls into my arms, pulling her blanket with her. She sinks into me and falls straight back into her dreams. The damned cat even joins the pile and curls up on Gabriel's legs.

I wrap my arms around her. Gabriel wraps his arms around us both.

And we all fall into the most blissful sleep together.

Chapter 2

The distant echo of Callie's giggle pulls me awake. I'm back in my bed, the blankets tucked tight beneath my chin and the soft breeze from the open window gliding over my face, bringing with it the fresh scent of the ocean. The birds call out their morning song, and the waves lap at the shore, creating a beautiful harmony. Gabriel's booming laugh has me smiling. And Callie's hysterical chortles have me beaming.

Now, that's a soundtrack I love to wake up to.

I sit and roll my neck free of the cramps from sleeping in a twisted ball of limbs on the floor with my family. Gabriel must have put me back to bed not long ago, and judging by the smell wafting up the stairs, he was ushered to the kitchen for breakfast shortly after.

The girl loves to eat.

I swing my legs over the side of the bed and take a series of deep breaths.

In... out...in...out.

I tell myself where I am. I tell myself who I'm with.

I tell myself that I'm safe.

That everyone is safe.

Every morning I do this. Almost as if to ground myself in my reality.

My heavenly reality.

I get to my feet.

Our bedroom is a good size and wonderfully homely. The cottage reminds me of the pictures in the books I would read when studying history. This realm froze in the fifteen hundreds. The same day Rebecca Hooper performed the spell which created it. A mirror image of the human world but containing within it all the magic in the universe. It started moving again after I completed the final spell at the final Bloodstone, but otherwise, we live in a world lost centuries ago to humans.

This cottage was the same one I lived in with Amara when we were both over here, pregnant with our children.

I gave birth in this very bed.

It's a Tudor home with high ceilings and wooden beams filled in with brick. Our roof is thatched, and every room has its own rustic fireplace and classic charm. The furniture is what I would call antique, but it's all brand-new.

I feel like I live in the history books but in the most idyllic version possible.

We have magic, after all. And knowledge. And you better believe we have plumbing, clean water, and fully functioning irrigation systems.

The whole of the left side of the bedroom wall is fitted with shelves. Gabriel stacked them with countless books he found whilst I was *"away"*. The rest of the walls are filled with sketches of us all, drawn from his memories, to keep my presence in the house for him and Callie. I'm in every single one, side by side with them as she grows from baby to toddler to child.

I grab the shirt Gabriel wore yesterday evening and slide it on as I do every day.

His clothes. His scent. My drug.

He ensures I have one each and every morning to wear. Even as I slide it on, I hear Hendrix.

"It ain't normal. You're always smelling that man and his clothes."

"Because he smells of home," I replied as we walked down the street towards the old Witch Museum in search of Rebecca Hooper's wedding ring.

That never happened. Not after I threw us all back in time and changed our destiny.

But yet, we remember it all. We remember the pain and loss we all endured. The sheer terror as we were annihilated by Theo's Hunters and the vigilantes.

And those memories of a life that never came into being refuse to leave us be.

We may not bear the scars on the outside. We sure as shit wear them on the inside.

I shake my head, ridding the words of the filthy vampire from my mind, and step out onto the landing.

Our home is nothing like we had in our old life. We have no electricity here, seeing as we have no need for it with magic and all it does is cause pollution and danger. We have no need to boast of wealth or standing. The Orchard was so grand and pristine. My Uncle's home was so cluttered and loud.

Our home is ours. It's perfect.

I pass through the landing, past Callie's bedroom full of her toys, past the guest rooms, which are used more often than they're not, and past the bathroom towards the stairs.

Below, there's a small lobby with a door to the left which leads into our lounge, complete with sofas, more books, games and a pool table the boys no doubt spent far too long building.

Ahead is the kitchen. And that is where I hear them.

I linger in the doorway and watch with amusement as Gabriel and Callie look up at the ceiling, laughing like lunatics at the pancake currently stuck above their heads. The stove is splattered with pancake mix and the large table in the very middle of the room is filled with fresh fruit.

Gabriel puts down the pan and spatula and takes hold of Callie's waist, lifting her high above his head.

'Get it,' he chuckles, reaching her higher. 'Go on! It's the best one we've made yet!'

She is laughing so hard her face is beet-red and she can hardly catch a breath, but she reaches up for it. Teasingly, he holds her just a little lower than she needs to be, making her giggle all the harder.

I can't help but join in. My laugh has Gabriel's eyes on me in an instant and they glisten with joy. Something as simple as a pancake stuck on the ceiling... it brings such happiness.

He lifts her higher and she grabs it. But it slips through her fingers and lands with a splat on Gabriel's forehead.

The room falls silent before we all explode in hysterics.

I walk over and peel it off him before dropping it in the sink and picking out the odd bit of batter from his hair.

Callie is now snorting.

'What are you doing to your poor daddy?' I ask, taking her and sitting her on my hip. 'And more importantly, what are you doing to my pancakes?'

She tries to explain how it got up there, but her laughs refuse to allow out a single word.

Gabriel leans over and we share a kiss.

'Good morning, Beautiful.'

'Good morning.'

'Sit. Breakfast is almost ready.' He gestures to the table, laid out for not just *us* to sit and eat but for others too.

And as if they were waiting to hear those words, the front door opens and in they come.

Same as every morning.

Collins holds open the door, letting his son, Finley, through first. As if there is any other choice. The kid's a wrecking ball of energy and comes charging in. His face is so full of excitement as he plonks his backside down at the chair he has claimed his own. Right beside Callie's. Each of them took their sweet time choosing which of the identical chairs they would claim as theirs forever and ever. They then proceeded to spend a day decorating them with paint and dried flowers before asking Gabriel to carve their names into the wood to really stake their claim.

Now Finley will forever have a place at our table, a fact he reminds us of daily. And one I will hold him to for the rest of my life.

Callie wriggles free of my arms and runs to sit beside him, keen to tell the story of the great pancake tragedy of this morning.

The next through the door is a rather tired-looking Amara, complete with six-month-old baby Lilah in her arms.

'Morning, Honey,' she beams, striding past Collins and handing him the baby. Her arms open wide and we hug.

The same as we do each and every morning when they come over for breakfast.

I think back to the time we sat talking about our future in the Arcane Realm. Amara said we would live next door to each other. That there would be a hole in the hedge between our gardens. But in reality, we never even put those hedges in.

We have a path lined with daffodils connecting our front door to theirs, and when that door opens each and every morning and she walks in with her family, I swear, the sun shines just that little bit brighter.

'You look like you had as much sleep as I did,' she yawns, stepping back to take a look at me. 'Nightmares still determined to keep you up?'

'No more so than your gorgeous little girl.' As Collins passes, I take my chance and reach out to take her. 'My turn for cuddles,' I grin.

Lilah's so small and obviously teething as she starts gnawing on my shoulder.

'Watch that. She'll soak through your shirt.' Collins yawns with extreme exaggeration as he heads over to Gabriel at the stove.

The two share a hug. The half-brothers who had no idea they were related for five entire centuries. They stood side by side through thick and thin. Through every trial. Every battle. Every loss and defeat.

And now they stand side by side to make their wives and children their morning pancakes.

And soon, we're all sat at the kitchen table together.

I hold Lilah as Amara and Collins eat and I watch as Callie, not so sneakily, drops some of her food on the floor for her kitten to enjoy. The children soon get bored, as children that age do when sat for too long, and they begin flicking blueberries at their dads to see who can hit them in the face first.

They both win with a bit of help from me as I use my Telekinesis to guide the projectile blueberries straight to both Gabriel's and Collins' foreheads.

'That's cheating,' Gabriel reprimands, taking a blueberry and flicking it in my direction.

'Natural advantage,' I correct.

He and Collins stand and clear the plates.

'Did you see him yesterday?' I ask Amara quietly as the guys talk about a fence that needs sorting in the sheeps' paddock at the far end of the field.

'No,' Amara replies, shaking her head apologetically. 'I sent Collins out to his usual haunts last night, but nothing.'

'I'm getting worried.'

'You shouldn't be worried. He does this a lot,' Amara insists, reaching over and taking Lilah, nodding to my plate of untouched food. 'Eat. Bias likes the quiet and sometimes he feels safer alone.'

'He shouldn't be on his own. What if he does something to himself?' I take another glance at the others, making sure that they're busy enough not to hear us. 'We all remember everything. Even though it never got a chance to happen, it did happen. We all know that. Bias has to live with centuries of horror. I know he wanted to end everything after I forced him to fix his Break. What if-'

'He needs time to deal with things his own way. He's not ready to forgive himself yet. Not that he should,' she adds with a mutter.

'You don't understand. Being Broken... you're not re-sponsible for what happens. It took going through it myself to really understand. Bias and Toby are not the same per-son. Hating him or blaming him would be like me blaming you for something Gabriel did.'

'What did I do?' Gabriel asks, picking a squashed blue-berry from his hair and peering over at us.

'Nothing,' we both reply together.

He raises his brow, knowing damn well I'm talking about something he wouldn't want me to be dwelling on.

And he waits, brow high and unyielding eyes boring into mine.

'Bias,' I concede.

'What about him?'

'Bias took off again,' Collins tells him as he pours the juice. 'I went to look for him last night, but he's gone.'

Gabriel takes a slow inhale and lets it out heavily. 'Did he leave a note?'

'Yep. The same old. "Gone to clear my head. Be back soon".'

'Do we know how long he's been gone this time?'

'At least three days,' I reply. 'After he came over for dinner and stayed the other night, he rushed off early in the morning and no one has seen him since.'

'He'll turn up,' Gabriel insists. 'It's what he does.'

'I hate the idea of him hiding away, filled with self-hatred and fear,' I reply, looking into nothing and recalling the fragile man I pulled out of Toby Smith in that cell. How he risked everything for me. Obeyed my dark requests even when it caused him to suffer. How he fought endlessly to keep me safe, to bring me back, to reunite me with the others. And how he suffered with the knowledge of what his dark side did when it was in control.

'Bias has bad days. He just needs to work through it in his own way.'

'Problem is, Gabriel, a bad day for people like us can be deadly,' I remind him. 'Once we suffer a Break, if we feel too much misery, we might lose everything.'

'Correction. Bias has a Break. Yours never got to happen, remember? And neither did mine.'

'We don't know that for sure. The memories are still inside us all. I could just as easily Break as much as he could. Or you. I don't want him on his own. I don't want any of us to ever-'

Gabriel slams his hand down on the counter. We all fall silent as we watch his mouth form a straight line and the muscles in his neck bulge.

'I'm done talking about this. Done!' His eyes flash with anger as I sit stunned in silence at his fury. 'I don't want to hear another mention of Breaks or Toby Smith or any other fucking Kendryk man for as long as I fucking live. Got that?!'

I've not seen him angry since we reunited.

I admit, it frightens me a little. Evident by how I just blink at him and feel the colour drain from my face.

'Gabriel...' Amara hisses, looking just as stunned as I feel. She glances at the kids and then me before stopping to glare at him once more. 'What on earth is wrong with you?! Don't you dare speak to her that way.'

His features soften and remorse at his outburst washes over him. As he goes to speak, Callie beats him to it.

'What's a Break?' she asks, looking up at us as she scratches behind Shadow's ear.

No one answers her question. No one knows what to say at all.

Gabriel goes to walk toward me. To speak.

I stand.

'Excuse me.' I scoop Callie up in my arms. 'The chickens need feeding.'

I leave the kitchen. Amara, Finley and Lilah follow. Amara glares at Gabriel and as he goes to say something, she waves her hand and sends several more blueberries at his face.

Collins snorts and hands him a towel.

'You kinda deserved that one, mate.'

Together, we head towards the chicken coop. Callie and Finley run ahead, giggling and playing.

The grass is damp with mildew and the smell of the ocean fills my senses. Our cottage is at the top of a cliff, set back a fair distance but close enough so we can see the ocean from our kitchen window. I stop to look at where an evergreen tree grows. One decorated with silver stars and hand-carved decorations.

Our permanent Christmas tree, forever standing tall.

They all planted it shortly after arriving here without me, and they've tended to it every day for the long five years I was away.

Five years.

Five fucking years.

The heavy ache in my heart at those lost years drags at my soul, leaving a weakness in its place for the dark thoughts to sneak in.

My hands tremble as my mind flashes with a series of violent images.

So much blood. So much death and torture.

So many faces, all snarling and shouting and threatening.

My whole life... just cruelty. So much goddamn cruelty.

Is Gabriel snapping at me all it takes to feel this terrible?

'You okay?' Amara asks as we walk.

'Fine.'

'I think I got him in the eye with a blueberry if that makes you feel any better.'

'A little,' I smile. 'It's okay. Gabriel can be angry. I know I am. Angry. Scared. Paranoid.' I look around us, at the world we now have as our own. 'I'm scared it will all come tumbling down. Gabriel is too. I know he is. Every time Gabriel looks at Bias, he goes rigid. Like he's getting ready to fight. I think that when Gabriel sees Bias, sometimes, he still sees Toby.' I look at her as we walk. 'I wonder if when he looks at me, if he sometimes sees *her*.'

'Her as in-'

'*Her*, with the white hair and lilac eyes. Blood on her skin and a soul as dark as death.' I gesture to myself. 'Her.'

'No. Absolutely not. No way. He's just the same as the rest of us. Scared to lose everything we've fought so hard for. He has a wife and daughter he adores, and he lost them both once before. Even the idea of losing you is too much to bear.' She glances back and grins. 'Case in point.'

I look over my shoulder and see Gabriel running after us.

'I'll sort the chickens. You sort your husband's attitude.' She gives my cheek a kiss and follows the kids as I wait for Gabriel.

'You can't yell at me like that,' I snap as he approaches. 'Not in front of Callie-'

He pulls me into his chest and seals his arms around me, burying my face into his shirt.

'I'm sorry. I should never have snapped at you like that. It was my fault. Completely mine. It was nothing to do with you at all and I was an arsehole for reacting the way I did.' His words spill out in quick succession before he leans down and kisses the top of my head. 'I'm so fucking sorry. I am so, so sorry.'

His arms tighten and he slowly sways from side to side.

'I just can't even think about it, you know?' he says quietly. 'The thought of losing you. The thought of losing myself or Bias again. The mere idea of it... I can't stand it. I can't, Lilly. But I shouldn't have snapped at you like that. Not after everything you've been through. Please forgive me.'

I give a single nod. Of course, I forgive him.

I peer up at him. His dark hair hangs over his ocean blue eyes as he meets my gaze. God, I fucking love those eyes.

'I'm sorry. I'm scared too. That's why we must look out for each other. We need to stay together.'

He plants a lingering kiss on my forehead.

'You're not going anywhere,' he says, as if reminding himself, me, and the universe, that he will not allow it. Not again. 'Neither am I, and neither is Bias. Please, don't talk about Breaks anymore. It's too painful.'

We stand there for a moment, watching the forever Christmas tree gently sway in the distance.

I have no idea if the Break still exists within Gabriel and me. Technically, this body never Broke and neither did his. Technically, I never had a relationship with Toby. I never got pregnant with his child, and he never did what he did to me in that barn on the Miller's farm. And the horrors that Gabriel faced when he became the Grey Cloak never come to pass either. Not for his body.

We all know it happened, though. We remember every bit of it.

But Bias, his Break *did* happen. It happened centuries ago. He feels it every day, scratching just beneath the surface. A constant promise that if it gets the chance, the monster of Toby Smith may one day return.

Bias fears his Break, just as much as I fear mine, and Gabriel fears his.

And that fear creates only more fear.

Bias is trying. I know that. The others know that too.

He dotes on Callie. He serves the community with all he has to offer.

But when he has a bad day, when it all gets too much, he goes. He disappears and hides away.

This is the third time he's taken off without a word since I got here.

And I worry that one day, we will find his body. That he will decide that the threat of Toby's return just isn't worth it, and he will end it all.

When I look at Bias, I don't see the man I once loved. I don't see the monster that was Toby Smith.

I see the young man who risked everything to save Gabriel from Hunters all those centuries ago. I see the innocent boy who suffered unimaginable horror in the cells of the Witch hunters before he lost his battle to keep his soul and fell into the darkness, forced to live in the shadow of wickedness.

'I'll go looking for Bias later,' Gabriel promises. 'I'm sure he's fine. Please, try not to worry. Okay?'

'Okay.'

I gasp as Gabriel's lips crash onto mine. His hands grip me tight as he pins me to him, his tongue caressing mine with ferocious passion as his heavy breaths mingle with mine.

I sink into him. His embrace. His passion. I feel his excitement starting to grow and press between my legs.

I grab at any part of him I can get to. His hair. His neck. His shoulders. His chest. I'm desperate to keep him as close to me as possible. To soak him up in all his glory.

'EEEWWWWWW!' Callie squeals from behind us. 'Daddy, stop sucking on Mummy's face!'

Gabriel clears his throat and steps aside, hiding his dirty smirk from her as she runs toward me.

Gabriel awkwardly readjusts himself out of her line of vision.

'Amara and Collins are babysitting for a couple of hours tonight,' he tells me in a seductive promise. 'You and I are having some alone time.'

'I'll hold you to that,' I whisper back.

Callie leaps into my arms.

'Can I come with you to the village?' Callie asks, full of excitement.

'We're not going to the village today, kiddo,' Gabriel replies. 'We're fishing. Remember?'

Her brow knits together. 'But Clara said I could come if I wanted.' She points towards the chicken coop.

'Clara?' I ask. 'Oh...'

Amara appears from around the hedges that section off that part of the garden, walking side by side with another.

Clara.

She's a Telekinetic witch. Pretty strong, too. Considering she had no idea she was a witch when she first came here. She's in her late forties and loves to wear the most flamboyant coloured dresses she can find. Her black hair is always in loose curls that reach her hips, and she has the warmest smile. She waves at us and Callie waves back.

But her eyes land on me, and I know something isn't right.

'Good morning,' Clara greets happily. 'I am so sorry to bother you this morning, but I was sent by the Council to ask you to attend a rather impromptu meeting today.'

'Is everything okay?' I ask.

'I'm sure it will be,' Clara says, glancing at Callie briefly, not wanting to say too much in front of her. 'Are you able to come?'

'Of course,' I reply, looking at Gabriel. 'We'll come.' I glance at Amara. 'Will you watch Callie?'

'Morning!' calls Collins, with a mouth full of toast as he heads our way. He stops at Amara's side. 'Everything okay?' he asks, seeing Clara here.

'There's a council meeting,' Gabriel tells him.

Collins stills and looks uneasy at his words but says nothing more as the kids are here.

'Can you watch Callie?' I ask Amara again.

'Well, if you don't mind,' Amara replies. 'We'll come to the village with you. We were planning on taking Finley to the school today so he can get a look at it before he starts next term. I can take Callie too? Let her have a look?'

I feel all their eyes on me.

'I think that's a great idea,' Gabriel replies.

I frown as he smirks. He knows I'm not sold on the idea of sending her to school. Or anywhere if it means her being out of my sight for more than ten minutes. He shows me that half-smile of his.

'An hour at the village, then we can come back and take her fishing as planned. What do you say?' He waits for my answer.

All of them look beyond hopeful that I'll concede.

'Fine,' I huff.

The lot of them visibly relax.

'This doesn't mean I'm saying yes to the whole school thing.'

'She's going to be an Arcane, Lilly,' Gabriel says, reaching over and taking Callie from my arms. They both beam at each other. 'She needs to be in school.'

'I do, Mummy,' Callie adds, nodding firmly. 'I need to play with my friends all day.'

'Yeah, yeah.' I turn to Clara. 'What time is the meeting?'

'Whenever you're ready. The Council are there already.' She clears her throat and looks around, her face suddenly blushing. 'Is erm... is Jensen here this morning?'

I spot Gabriel and Amara's little smirks.

'Not this morning, no. He didn't stay over last night. Does the Council need him too?' I ask, knowing full well that Dad has made it very clear that he wants nothing to do with politics, and he's in retirement. Unless he's needed, of course, then I'm sure he'd be first into battle.

But he's had enough of all that and just wants to be a dad to me and a grandad to Callie.

Clara, however, is very keen on being something to him too.

And I know he feels the same. A couple of shy teenagers, I swear.

'Can we *whoosh*?' Callie asks.

I look at Gabriel, who nods.

'Yes, baby,' I laugh. 'We can *whoosh*.'

We all gather outside. Gabriel holds Callie in his arms, a sight I will never get tired of, and in a flurry of wind, I summon my magic and send us all to the village.

As Callie says, we *whoosh*.

As soon as we arrive, we're welcomed with excited gasps and enthusiastic greetings as those who live in the village rush towards us.

A couple of them shake Gabriel's and Collins' hands. Children rush to see Callie and Finley. And all of them offer me a bow and their thanks and gratitude.

Something I have asked them repeatedly not to do.

Amara and I are offered the food they have in their baskets or a sip of their lemonade or juice. We politely refuse, but I ensure I speak to each and every witch who chooses to speak to me.

Whilst I was away, Gabriel and the others built up several wonderful communities here. This village is the main one. There are also settlements by the coast. Some in the woodlands. And some witches choose to travel, exploring the country or the world.

As the witches arrived in the Arcane Realm, most of them flocked to England, keen to join together and start a new world as a united front. The Nomads were spread far and wide. The Traitors too. But with the knowledge of the truth behind both Grayson's and Theo's motives and how they happily murdered them all to serve their own selfish purposes, they soon aligned themselves with us.

With Gabriel.

He took charge and made this place a home for thousands upon thousands.

'Gabriel!' greets a familiar voice. A young man steps through the growing crowd and holds out his hand. Gabriel shakes it fondly. 'Thank you so much for coming.' He looks at me and gives a respectful bow. 'Lilly. A real honour.'

'Good morning, Ash. How are you?'

'All the better for seeing you.'

Ash's light brown hair is flecked with grey, odd as he's only a few years older than me, and his eyes always feel familiar. Like I've seen them a hundred times before, but we only met six months ago when I first came here.

He puts on a large smile for Callie.

'And hello to you too, young lady. My, my. Aren't you getting big?! You must have doubled in size since I last saw you.'

'You only saw me last week,' she chuckles.

Ash turns to Clara.

'Morning, Mum,' he greets, leaning in and giving her a kiss on her cheek.

'Good morning, darling,' Clara replies.

'Thank you for passing over our message.' Ash turns to me expectantly. 'Shall we?'

I let go of Callie, and Collins takes her hand.

I kiss her, as does Gabriel, and I watch Amara and Collins take her through the village.

With a slight nudge from Gabriel, I follow Ash down the cobbled streets, through the bustling markets and past the homes of the witches who now live here, filling up this once empty world.

I remember walking through here when only Amara, Rebecca and I lived in this place. I remember the deafening silence. The still summer day that repeated again and again.

Now there's a wonderful breeze and the streets are full of life. Three children run past us, using their Telekinesis to play wooden sword fights with each other.

Two women stand at the door of a bakery, handing out freshly baked bread to all who ask for it.

No one here is hunted or persecuted. No one goes hungry or cold. No one is left to struggle alone.

Everyone chips in. Everyone is equal. Currency is not needed here. Everyone pitches in with the work, whether that's growing food, making clothes, caring for the children, or educating them.

And that is thanks to Gabriel and the group of witches who stood at his side when they first arrived here.

Those who later became *The Council*.

It's a group of twenty people from every background possible. Those born Nomads, Traitors and those who believed they were human and ended up here quite unexpectedly.

I wonder if perhaps that is what this is about.

Those who arrived in this realm without any knowledge of their heritage. Of the magic that lurked in their blood, lost to the sands of time.

Ash is upfront, storming ahead and too far away to ask without causing worry to the happy faces that surround us.

Many hold out their hands for me to shake. Many continue to offer a bow. Many give their friends a nudge, pointing me out.

So when we approach the town hall and step inside, I feel relieved to have fewer eyes on me.

That is until we walk into the council meeting room, where dozens of people suddenly stand and face me in silence.

'Oh... this can't be good,' I grumble, looking up at Gabriel as he stands beside me.

Our hands grip each other a little tighter as the door closes behind us.

Chapter 3

'Are you certain?' I repeat, almost pleadingly. 'Is there no possibility that they are just... travelling?'

'I'm afraid not,' Ash replies. 'There were definite signs of a struggle at their home. Several other council members saw blood and scuff marks when they attended late last night. And none of their personal effects were gone, so if they did leave, they took nothing with them.' Ash shakes his head and knots his fingers together. 'I'm afraid that Mrs Gower and her grandson were almost certainly attacked. And taken.'

'And this is in addition to the three others who haven't been seen for the last week?' I ask, looking at the group surrounding me. 'How can we lose five people in a week, and Gabriel and I are only hearing about it now?'

'There were no signs of distress with the others,' Ash says. 'Ethan McGuire said he was going to hunt deer for a few days, and the Willow couple often goes exploring. They haven't been seen for almost a week and that is very unusual for them.' He turns to two men by the door. 'It is thanks to their diligence that we are finding out about this now. Thank you for bringing it to our attention.'

The two men nod.

'They probably got lost, or maybe they decided to stay longer in the wilderness?' Gabriel's words are less than convincing to himself or to the rest of us.

'No. We must assume the worst and start looking for them immediately,' I announce. 'What do they do for the community?'

'McGuire helps to hunt for food. Mr Willow works the farms and Mrs Willow assists with the management of the library,' says Clara. 'And Mrs Gower is elderly. She occasionally helps by knitting blankets and such. Her grandson is twelve. He's at school.'

'Has there been any further disturbances with "The Stolen"?' I ask. 'Could they be involved?'

'Well, that is why we wanted you to come here today,' Ash says. 'Things with that lot are tense at the best of times. They don't come too close unless they intend to start trouble. We want your permission to go and enquire about our lost people with their camp, but as I said-'

'Things are tense,' I nod. 'They will not be forthcoming if they are up to something, but in the same regard, if they were making another play for the impossible, we would know. There's no point in taking people hostage and holding them to ransom if you're not planning on telling the people you intend to blackmail.' I look at Gabriel as he awaits my word. 'We will go and see The Stolen with you. If our people are there, we will find them.'

'Are you certain?' Gabriel asks. 'They don't really like you.'

'Please,' I scoff. 'It's people *liking* me that I'm not used to. Who here can give Gabriel and me a clear visual image of the missing witches?'

'I know them well,' says a lady member of the council. 'The Willows have-'

'If you just think about them, we'll see them,' I interject, reaching out my hand. 'As long as you don't mind us using our Mental powers on you?'

'It would be an honour,' she says with a humble bow.

We take her hands, and she shares with us an image of the missing members of the village.

After, I look at the three members of the council who linger closely together at the side.

'You three are from The Stolen's camp, is that right?' I ask.

'Technically, we are. Only by circumstance,' says the youngest. A blonde girl in her early twenties. 'But as you know, we embraced our change in fortune a year or so after arriving. We embrace our magic.'

'You're Megan, right?'

She nods.

'Would you come along with us?' I ask her. 'They may feel more at ease if they see you with us. See that we haven't sacrificed you or something stupid.'

'Me?'

'Only if you don't mind. I would ask Clara to come. But last time she went in there, she sent a pile of fox shit into the leader's face.'

The whole room snorts with laughter.

'I warned him to stop calling me a whore,' Clara shrugs. 'Not my fault he kept on at me. Besides, Ash and I were never a part of that group. As soon as we arrived here, we sought Gabriel out and made our allegiances crystal clear. Megan is much better suited to go than I.'

'Do you mind?' I ask Megan once more. 'Your mother is still there, I believe. Will you be okay?'

'Of course,' she replies, nodding with wide and surprised eyes. 'To help you would be a great honour, but I don't expect my presence will help. I'm a deserter in their eyes. A traitor. And my mother has always been a bitch. I highly doubt that has changed much.'

'Fox poo,' Clara declares, waving her hand in the air and showing the girl a kind wink. 'I'm telling you. It's the best way to go.'

'It's settled then. We'll go now and see if they have anything to do with this or we will rule them out.' I look up at Gabriel, waiting for his confirmation that I have made the right choice.

He just winks, proudly watching me.

'Whoosh?' he asks me.

'Whoosh,' I agree.

The young girl clears her throat.

'Whoosh?' she asks anxiously. 'What's "whoosh"?'.

We arrive on the outskirts of the woodland that belongs to the group called 'The Stolen.'

Fucking idiots, is what I call them.

All but Gabriel, Ash and I land in a disoriented heap on the floor. We help them up and get them steady on their feet.

'I see,' Meghan chuckles nervously, dusting off her clothes. 'So that's a Whoosh.'

As a precaution, I send a stream of my red fire to the ground and watch the flames swirl and morph, creating two of my fire wolves.

'Just in case,' I shrug as Gabriel, Ash, and Megan watch them prowl around them before coming to me and nuzzling my hands.

Their fire never burns me. Not how it would burn anyone else. It's a comforting warmth on my skin. A reassurance.

'That's incredible,' Megan gasps, reaching out her hand to touch them.

Gabriel grabs her wrist, stopping her.

'I wouldn't. Lilly can touch her flames, no one else. Not unless you want to be scarred for life.'

'They're... incredible!' she admires. She holds out her palm. The faintest flicker of a dull flame awakens on her skin. 'How do you do it?'

'By being the Arcane,' Gabriel replies. 'Come on.'

The magical capabilities of the coven are... limited. Advanced magic such as transportation or extreme control over a fire that enables separate entities is rare.

So rare, only I can do it.

Arcane Witch perks, I guess.

So when they see it, they are often awe-struck.

As we make our way closer to the group who refuse to live with us, refuse to acknowledge their heritage, and refuse to get over the fact that they are not human, the first thing to hit us is the smell.

'Christ...' Gabriel sneers, burying his mouth and nose in the crook of his elbow. 'What is that?'

'Sewage,' Megan replies with a grimace. 'And unwashed clothes, people and their rotting food.'

As we step through the trees and come into view of the clearing where they make camp, we halt, and I call out.

'Hello? We're not here to hurt anyone. We just came to talk. Is there someone here-' I hold my hand up, stopping a rock mid-air as it comes hurtling at my head. 'I said we're not here to hurt anyone, but if you throw another rock at us, that may change. Come out.'

I drop the rock to the ground as my wolves step ahead and snarl.

From the makeshift tents and shacks, from behind trees, people start to emerge.

They all look so afraid. So angry.

So sick.

They wear rags, pieces of cloth that are crudely held together by rope. Many have no shoes, and their skin is filthy and grey. A few fires are lit and the smell of cooking meat wafts through the air, but hardly enough to distract from the utter stench of their filth.

Many of the kids are crying and coughing. They're painfully thin. It's enough to make me want to scream.

A tall, gaunt and rigid-looking man steps out from the crowd, wearing something that resembles a suit from his previous life. I imagine it was once a lovely suit. I expect he wore it to his job, proud of the expensive silk tie that now hangs loose and tattered around his neck.

That, and the large, crudely carved crucifix that hangs beside it.

They all have crucifixes on them. From what I understand, the bigger it is, the higher their rank.

And his is the biggest.

He stops and spits at my feet.

'Witch whore. You are not welcome–'

'Silence,' Gabriel orders, his eyes black. The man falls quiet in an instant. 'And if anyone else dares speak to my wife like that, you will not enjoy what comes next.'

'Calm, my love,' I whisper, taking his arm and pulling him back to my side. I look at the rest of them and try to smile, which is hard as I loathe them for allowing themselves and their families to live this way. 'I know that you do not wish for us to be here,' I call out to the rest of the group. 'And believe me, I wish that you were not here either. You know that there is no need for you to be living like this. You are all welcome at the village.'

They shuffle their feet and scoff at my words.

'Then you are welcome to claim another village for yourselves,' I offer. 'The entire world is yours if you want it. You are free to go wherever you like. Up north, there are many, many towns with homes lying empty. You don't need to live like this.'

This isn't the first time I have been here. Nor the second or third. I've come many times, offering them something more than this hell as a life.

Each time I get the same response. Disgusted looks. Vile insults. Threats.

Witch whore. Satan's puppet. Heathen. Murderer.

I've heard them all.

Not a single person in this camp wanted to be sent to the Arcane Realm. They all believed themselves human. They hated magic. They hated witches. They hate themselves and refuse to accept their magic or their place here.

The only thing they claim to love is God. And because I have "stolen" them, I have also shunned them from their God. Damned their eternal souls to the pits of hell.

Blah. Blah. Blah.

Many wear binding spells around their wrist. When I discovered one man attempting to create a Brand, I lost my shit entirely and stole any knowledge of the practice from his head and from anyone else's who thought they knew how to do it.

I didn't even know I could do that. But I was so enraged when I saw the Brand that I lunged at the man, grabbed his head and dug in deep. I spoke to the Arcane Realm that day. I demanded this never be allowed again, and it obeyed. It guided me into his mind. It guided me straight to his knowledge. And it let me pluck it from his mind and everyone else's.

I've done that before. Spoken to the magic in this realm. When I commanded it to save me after the second spell, it sent me here to have Callie in safety.

And again, when I harnessed its power and it sent me back to my previous self so I could complete the final spell.

And then when I saw that branding iron. I vowed never to let another be held captive like that, so I abolished all knowledge of it from every mind in this place.

It knocked me out for a week after.

Scared Gabriel half to death.

My magic may be mighty. My knowledge extensive.

But this body has only had access to it for six months.

It's not strong enough to wield what I'm capable of yet.

But it will be.

The man, complete with an oversized crucifix, steps forwards and starts reciting scripture. Something about the hand of God.

I'm distracted by another. At the very back of the group, a woman holds a baby, rocking it relentlessly as it wails and wails. It's a cry full of pain and suffering.

Gabriel nudges me and pulls me back to the matter at hand.

The man stops his recital and glares.

'We have come to offer you help once more,' I call out. 'Food. Access to our medical care and-'

'You have come to try and seduce our souls into the depths of hell,' crucifix man barks. 'We have told you before, Witch. We have no intention of succumbing to your depraved, heathenistic rituals.'

'You live in filth out of stubbornness,' I state plainly. 'You live in hunger and burn the food we send you. You die of sickness when relocating and accepting your true nature will spare you any suffering.'

'You are the one who kills us. Starves us,' he argues.

'We have done nothing but try to help you.'

'You stole us,' accuses a woman from the crowd, causing others to murmur in agreement. 'You took us from our homes. Our families. Your duty is to return us to the Human Realm. To save our souls before it is too late.'

'You know I can't do that,' I repeat for the hundredth time. 'The Veil is sealed and can not be reopened. Even if it could, you would return to a human world that would shun you because you are not human. Your children are not human, and the Hunters who still reside over in the Human Realm will hunt you down and kill you.'

'We don't want your magic,' spits another. 'Keep it. Our Lord God, our heavenly father, will save us soon, and he will burn you and all your Satan-worshipping sluts-'

'I'm going to stop you there. If you can't come up with any other insults except whore and slut, I'm not even going to bother discussing this with you.' I look beyond them, to those lingering at the sidelines. To the ones who are noticeably thinner than those yelling insults. To those whose clothes are barely clothes at all.

The lowest of this self-loathing cult of witches who believed they were human and long to return to a world of politics, war, pollution and persecution.

'My invitation for you to take up residence in a town is open to you all.' I assure them. 'My offer of peace is always in place. We did not steal you from your life. Any pain you are feeling at being here is unintentional, and I am sorry. But know this. You will never return to the human world. The Veil is closed for good and will never again re-open. So instead of living in squalor, I implore you, just say the word and we will gladly help you.'

'In exchange for our souls!' yells the sharp-looking man to the rest of the crowd. 'She will feed your living soul to her satanic master if you allow her. Do not be tempted by her beauty and sensuality. She is nothing more than Lucifer's harlot.'

Gabriel snorts and bursts out laughing. He's the only bloody one. Everyone else looks ready to either run, faint or fight.

'Sorry,' he chokes as I glare at him. 'I just... where does he come up with this shit?'

'You are not helping.'

'Sorry, Lucifer's harlot.' He clears his throat and forces on a straight face. 'I'm good.'

Rolling my eyes, I look back at the crowd.

'Some of my people have gone missing,' I declare, keen to move this on. 'Five, in fact. I will give you one chance now to tell me if you know anything of their whereabouts. If you have them in some idiotic attempts to force my hand in reopening the Veil, I must warn you that not only is that a pointless endeavour but a very foolish one. I will not allow any harm to come to peaceful people, so if you have taken them, speak now. Hand them over and we will leave. If you do not and I discover they are here or you know where they are, then I will not be happy.' My wolves snarl and dig their claws into the ground. My magic peaks and the ground trembles a little, just to show them that I mean fucking business. 'Not happy at all.'

'You have ten minutes before we start searching your camp ourselves,' Gabriel states.

'We don't have any of your demons here.' The woman that snaps her words is one of the older ones and wears a large, crude crucifix around her neck. As she starts calling us every name under the sun, I can't stop watching the young mum at the back of the crowd, still rocking her small baby who is shrieking.

Her eyes land on mine. They're so tired and worried. They are full to the brim with tears, and as her gaze lands on mine, I see her lip tremble.

'Oh, I can't deal with this anymore,' I hiss. My eyes go black, and I look at the group in the middle with the largest crucifixes, all throwing insults and hatred at us. 'Go the fuck to sleep. Now.'

As soon as I speak, they fall to the floor with their eyes closed.

The others lingering at the edges, unsure and frail-looking, I left alone.

'You shouldn't have done that,' Ash says with a half-amused chuckle. 'But now they're out, can we at least wash them? They stink.'

I make my way towards the young mother, who staggers back a few steps as I approach. I hold out my hands.

'Give me your baby.'

'N-no... please... don't hurt-'

'She's sick. I can hear it in her cry. I see her flustered cheeks and the clamminess of her skin. She's in pain. Give her to me, or I will take her from you.'

The others around her watch in uncertainty and some shake their head, urging her not to hand over the infant.

But she's a mum. And most mums wouldn't care who the hell helped their child if they were suffering.

She hands me the child. I feel the fever through the blanket. I lower myself to the floor and rest the little girl on my legs before unwrapping her blanket. Gabriel kneels beside me and watches as I feel her little tummy.

'What other symptoms has she had?' I ask.

'Erm... she... she... her poo has had blood, and she is sick when she feeds.'

I channel my Physical magic, just as Collins has been teaching me. I send it out like a ripple from my fingertips and feel the resistance in her belly. I look at Gabriel.

'She has a blockage.'

'Good job you're here then, hey?' he says calmly. He gets to his feet. 'I'm borrowing one of your wolves if you don't mind,' he says as I focus on the little girl squirming before me. 'We'll start searching the camp as you do your thing here.'

I nod and press my fingers into her stomach, sending my power through her.

Her cries ease to a hiccup, and when I open my eyes, she's calm and quiet, looking up at me with the remnants of tears in her sweet little brown eyes. Her tiny fingers grab at my hair before she tries to shove it in her mouth.

'There,' I smile, gently retrieving my curls from her vice-like grip. 'All better.'

The young mother scoops her up, utterly stunned into silence as she looks at her happy, pink and babbling baby. Already so much healthier and happier.

'Thank you,' she gasps, pinning her babe to her chest. 'Oh, thank you.'

'It's my pleasure,' I assure her. 'And it would be my plea-sure to please, please let me help you get out of here.' I glance back at the sleeping mass in the centre of the camp. The camp leaders. 'They're wrong about us. We're not evil. We have no interest in your souls. And you and your children do not deserve to live like this.' I look at her again. 'Your baby would have died if I had not come here today. This is all so unnecessary.'

I wait and feel such relief when she nods.

As she does, others come forward, and within a few minutes, a group has gathered.

Not as many as I would like, but at least twelve of them.

The others remain firm, standing between their sleeping elders and us.

Gabriel arrives back with the others and shakes his head.

'They're not here, and no one knows anything about their disappearances,' he says, sliding his hands in his pockets and resting his gaze on the small group huddled together. 'What did I miss?'

'They're returning to the village with us. They will need housing, clothes, and food. And an evaluation of their powers.'

Gabriel nods and looks at Ash, who gives a little bow at my words.

'I will ensure they are settled as soon as we return,' he promises.

I stand, but the young mother reaches out and takes my arm. Looking up at me, she takes an anxious breath.

'You are missing people?' she asks.

'Yes. Do you know something about it?'

'We're missing some people too,' she says quietly, glancing at the others who tut and shake their heads, muttering the words sinner and traitor. 'In the last two months or so, people have gone missing.' She nods to the sleeping elders. 'They said they had joined you. That they were lost to hedonism and darkness. My father was one of them.'

I turn to Gabriel. He shakes his head.

'No. None of your people have come to us. And I'm sorry to say there is no hedonism or darkness in the village. But there is sanitation, food, clean clothes, health care and acceptance.' He offers her his hand, and she takes it, letting him help her to her feet.

'How many have gone missing?' I ask.

'I'm... I'm not sure. More than ten, I would say. That and...'

'And?'

'Well, we've been finding dead animals a lot.' She looks towards the distant hillside. 'Several miles away in that direction. I heard the elders talking. They said horses and cattle were found and looked as if they had been slaughtered by something. All carved up and stuff. They said it was your people.'

'No. Not us. We would never do that.' I sigh and look at the others as they share a nervous glance. But scaring these people is the last thing I want to do. Especially after some of them finally agreed to come back with us. 'We'll look into it,' I assure her. I turn to the others. 'No sign of our people at all?' I ask hopefully. They all shake their heads. Even my wolves do. So I face the rest. 'To those who wish to come with us today, collect your belongings. We're leaving in five minutes.'

They all just stand there, looking at me like I'm insane.

'They're wearing all their belongings,' Gabriel whispers in my ear. 'I think they're good to go.'

So be it.

'Anyone else want to come?' I offer. They all shuffle back. 'As you wish. We will continue to deliver food, clothes and fresh water to you. If you all choose to burn it, then that's on you, but I will do what my conscience tells me to do. Are there any who need medical attention?'

A few shift on their feet.

'You have five minutes to come and see me before we leave. I will ask for nothing in return. If anyone wishes to come to us for help with anything in the future, they can. If your children are sick, you bring them to the village. Even if you continue to refuse magical help, we have medicine that will help. That will save lives. The lives of your children.'

'We do not need your heretic interventions!' snaps an elderly woman.

'Then *you* don't have to have them. But that baby did today. She needed it, or her mother would have woken up tomorrow to her corpse lying in her crib. That child's death would have been on your conscience. On your soul. And when you die after the long life that you got to live, if you do meet this God of yours, you can explain to him how you let children die because you're a fucking cunt!'

The last word I yell, and it echoes all around us.

I reach out my hand, my eyes black and my Mental magic summoning the sleeping back to the world of the living. They look around, confused and on high alert.

'I will return,' I cut in before anyone can say a word. 'I will just appear, and if I discover you are keeping people from the help they need, there will be consequences.' I take a step towards them, and they all cower back, shuffling away from me in the dirt. And so they should. 'Make no mistake. If you are willing to let babies die in agony because of your closed-minded discrimination and religious delusions, I will take those children from you. They are a privilege. They are not your right. They are not your possession; they are your family. They are living, breathing, feeling souls, and I will not allow them to suffer because of you. If you do not fulfil the obligations you have to them, then I will. You do not want to be here. I get that. We did not want to be in your world either, but this is how it is. Refuse your magic if you want. But I will not allow any more needless suffering.

So I leave you with this to consider.' I glance at Gabriel. It's something we have discussed at length. 'An island.'

'What?' asks their leader, pushing himself to his feet.

'One to call your own. If you want it, it will be a place of no magic. I have seen the island. There are houses. Fresh water supplies. Wild animals to hunt and good earth for crops. If you want it, it is yours. And you will get no interference from us if that's what you wish.'

The offer is tempting. I can see it in his eyes as he looks at his squalor-filled home.

'Let me know when you have decided.' I look at the others. The ones still at the edges. 'You. You let me know. You don't need to live in their shadow. This world is yours. Claim it.'

'Send us home,' the leader snarls. 'You sent us here. SEND US BACK!'

Gabriel takes a menacing step toward him. I hold his wrist and keep him at my side.

'You miss your old life,' I tell him. 'You miss the power you had at work in that shiny office in the city. You miss the big house you owned. The trophy wife you fucked around on.'

His eyes blink quickly.

'Oh yeah, I know it all. I see your mind as clearly as I see the piss you're so desperately trying to hold in. And you know what you miss most? More than everything else? Do you know what he misses so much that he cries himself to sleep at night?' I ask the rest. 'Is it his church? Is it his family? No.' I shake my head and laugh. 'It's the internet. It's porn. Your leader is addicted to pornography, and he can think of nothing else except wanking off to videos of gang bangs and foot fetish videos.'

Those I came with scoff and laugh.

'But please, keep preaching about our dirty, deviant and sadistic way of life whilst you lie in the filth, pulling on your dick to distant memories of teenage girls getting fucked in every hole for your viewing pleasure.'

He lowers his face. Good move, because I really want to smack it.

'So,' I call out. 'If you need my magic to heal you, come see me now. For those coming with us, speak to Ash. Otherwise, I suggest you stay quiet and stay out of my way.'

Gabriel rests his hand on my back and whispers in my ear.

'I am so fucking proud of you, wife. So proud and extremely turned on.'

'Well, there was mention of some hedonism,' I grin back, looking at the small line of people shuffling towards me. 'Now excuse me, husband. I have some healing to do. Try and get more to come back with us, will you? Especially ones with children.'

'I'm on it, Beautiful.'

Chapter 4

We arrive back in the village via a large *'Whoosh'* as sweet Callie calls it. The twelve that decided to leave The Stolen behind were joined by six more. And I'm thrilled to see many of the babies and children are amongst them.

They all gasp and squeal as they land, tumbling to their backsides as they meet the ground. They quickly jump to their feet, holding their children or each other close.

Everyone in the village turns to face us, their eyes wide as they take in the sight of the downtrodden who join us.

'My goodness!' gasps one of the women at the bakery, grabbing a basket of bread and cakes as she rushes over to them. 'You all look half-starved! Here, eat!' She looks at her friend. 'Fetch milk and water, would you? They need to drink. And ask Gregory to get some fruit.'

The new arrivals look at the offering with concern, but the smell of freshly baked goods is damn near impossible to turn away when you're that hungry. They take the bread. They devour it. Others approach them, offering drinks. Blankets. Fruit. Milk for the children. The young mother whose baby I saved looks at me with tears in her eyes and a trembling lip.

'Thank you,' she says, seeing for herself that there is no evil here.

'Now, if only the other nutters would see that we're here to help. Not eat their fucking souls,' Gabriel huffs.

'They will. If not, and if they refuse to move somewhere they can live properly, then we take the children from them and send them to the island whether they like it or not.'

'Harsh.'

'No. Not for the children who are living in shit and going to bed hungry because of their parents' stupidity. I wish someone would have come to get me and save me from the adults that destroyed my life. I won't let that happen here. Not if I can stop it.' I turn to Ash. 'I believe there are some houses on the north side of the village that are vacant?'

He nods.

'Ensure they are close together. They will feel safer being with familiar faces. And ensure that they have food and water as well as clean clothes. And evaluate their magics. We need to know who has what so we can organise their training.'

He bows.

'Before you leave,' Ash says as I go to do just that. 'I wanted to offer an invitation for dinner soon. For you two and for Callie, of course. My girlfriend would absolutely love to meet you.'

'Erm, sure. We'll set something up.'

'Great. I would love to host you. Me and my girlfriend both.'

Ash smiles and turns his entire focus on the new arrivals.

'I've heard a lot about this girlfriend,' Gabriel mutters quietly. 'But no one has seen her. I'll be interested to see if she's real.'

'Fake girlfriends are the least of my concerns. I have to get back to Callie,' I tell Gabriel. 'I need her in my arms right now.'

He follows me as I head toward the school.

'The Stolen don't have the missing people. And the young mother said they are missing people too. Will you stay and ask her about it a little more?'

'Of course,' he agrees as we walk up the path to the school. 'I'll speak to family members and friends too. See if we're missing something. And I'll send a team to where the animal carcasses were found. See what's going on there.'

We step through the school courtyard and see some children sitting with a teacher. They surround a pile of logs and each takes a turn in trying to set them alight. They must be Elemental fire witches. When the youngest girl creates a successful flame, they all cheer.

'Good job, kid!' I call over.

Her mouth falls open as her friends all whisper about the Arcane Witch being here and speaking to them.

The main doors open, and Amara and Collins emerge. Along with Finley and Callie, each with a cookie in their hand and chocolate smeared all over their faces.

Now that's a glorious fucking sight.

The woman who teaches the young ones stands beside the children, smiling and making them both laugh so wonderfully.

I stop for a moment and think.

'What is it, Beautiful?' Gabriel asks.

'The missing. Find out what realms of magic they have access to. What families they are connected to. Were they with the Nomads, or were they with Dad?'

'Why? You think it matters?'

'Maybe. Knowledge is power. I want to know where our people are. Since you settled them and set up the council, nothing like this has happened. I don't like that this is happening now. After I get back? After my realms of magic have all nearly returned? I don't like it.' I shake my head. 'Not at all.'

'*MUMMMMMYYYYY!*'

'Hi, baby girl,' I greet, opening my arms for Callie as she bounds towards me.

I take her in my arms and let out a deep sigh, relieved to have her back.

Amara and Collins join us.

'How did it go?' Amara asks.

'As well as it could have.'

'Collins,' Gabriel asks. 'Would you mind staying with me for a bit? I could use some help.'

'Sure, man,' Collins replies, shovelling a cookie into his mouth. 'Whatever you need.'

'You erm...' Gabriel hesitates for a minute but decides to ask the question. 'At Bias's place. Was anything off?' he asks.

'Off?' Collins repeats.

'Did it all look normal? Any signs of trouble or anything?'

'Nope. Everything was as it usually is. He left a note that said he'll be back in a few days. Same as usual when he takes off.'

I feel my heart start to pick up a beat or two. 'You don't think Bias is in trouble, do you?' I ask hesitantly.

'No.' Gabriel shakes his head. 'He's more than capable of handling himself. I'm sure he's fine. I just wanted to double-check. You sure you don't want to stay?' Gabriel asks me.

'I'm pretty tapped out,' I tell him. 'Getting a bit of a headache. Can you guys cope?'

'Of course, my love.' He kisses my forehead. 'I'll be back by sunset.'

'Are we going fishing now?' Callie asks, cookie crumbs flying from her lips.

'Yes,' I chuckle.

'Enjoy the rest of your day,' Gabriel says. 'And say hello to your old man for me.'

'Will do.'

He leans in and kisses us both.

'I'll see you later, Beautiful.'

'You better.'

'Bye, Daddy,' Callie sings, still entangled around me like a vine.

'Bye, my sweet girl.' He lands her with another kiss and then takes my chin in his hands. 'I absofuckinglutely love you.'

'Love you more.'

'Impossible. If you need me...'

'I'll send for you. I promise.'

He looks deep into my eyes.

'Try and take it easy for the rest of the day. You're still building up your stamina and using too much magic too soon will hurt you. Your eyes are a little bloodshot.'

'One final whoosh home,' I assure him. 'Then I promise it will be a magic-free zone.'

He steps back as Amara and the kids get closer. I watch him walk away, deep in conversation with Collins about what has happened.

'Can we go see Grandpa now?' Callie asks.

'God, yes.' I summon my magic. 'Let's go see Grandpa.'

Chapter 5

We arrive back at the cottage in a whoosh. One Callie declares loudly as she runs around the permanent Christmas tree with her hands in the air.

We quickly stop inside and make a picnic basket before heading back out and making our way towards the woodland at the bottom of the hill. The two kids run ahead, waving sticks above their heads and singing some made-up song about mermaids and unicorns whilst discussing at length how much fun it will be when they finally get their magic or how great the school is.

Amara and I follow behind, with Amara carrying Lilah on her front in a wraparound carrier made of cloth.

'So no one has any ideas where they went?' she asks after I tell her exactly what happened in the meeting.

I shake my head.

'Apparently not. Gabriel and Collins are staying there to do some digging. I'm sure they will find something.'

'I kind of hope not,' she adds, looking down at Lilah. 'I'm personally hoping that they all snuck off together in secret, in some kind of love nest situation.'

'I'm not holding out much hope for that scenario, I'm afraid.'

'It's just...' she groans loudly. 'You've only been here a few months. It's time you relaxed. I think it's safe to say that you have earned a peaceful retirement.'

'Not sure I get to retire. Being the Arcane and all.' I look ahead to Callie and feel that swell of guilt that enjoys haunting me. 'If there's something shady going on, we'll put a stop to it and carry on with our lives. It's what we do. In the meantime...' I take a long and deep inhale, enjoying the world around me in all its glory. 'I don't think I will ever get used to how clean the air is here,' I smile. 'And I cannot stop looking up at the stars at night. It's so clear without the pollution. The kids are so lucky to have known nothing but this.'

'Has Gabriel mentioned anything more about having another baby?'

'Not since I almost choked to death on the sandwich I was eating when he first asked me about it,' I reply. 'No.'

'You're still not keen?'

'Maybe one day. But to be honest, I doubt it.' I watch Callie up ahead. 'She will come into her powers soon, and everything will change for her. Being an Arcane is so dangerous. I feel terrible that she will have to deal with all the shit that goes along with it. I'm not sure I want to subject anyone else to that if I don't have to.'

'Her experiences with the Arcane power won't be the same as yours. You need to remember that. She will have the best teachers. The greatest support and advice. She'll have you.'

'Either way, whatever is stopping Gabriel from having kids is staying that way for now. He can have it magically healed if we ever change our mind, but as you said, I've only been here a few months. I'm still not... I'm not entirely settled yet. I keep thinking something is going to tear me away or come after us. I just don't have the inner strength to add another baby into that yet. Especially if something is stirring and there's someone out there stealing witches. Never mind the creepy cult in the woods who keep trying shit to provoke me into sending them back to the human world.'

'All very fair points,' she laughs with a nod.

We carry on, watching the two kids clamber up a fallen log and balance their way along it. Finley reaches back and takes Callie's hand, keeping her steady as she stumbles a little. I love how he's always looking out for her. It's so adorable.

'You and Gabriel okay after he snapped at you this morning?' she asks.

'We're fine. He's just tired and on edge. Neither of us are getting a lot of sleep.'

'Like that, huh?' she smirks, wagging her eyebrows at me.

'Not quite,' I chuckle. 'I had another nightmare last night and ended up in Callie's room again. It's a wonder Gabriel hasn't tied me down to the bed yet. He's spent every night so far in the most uncomfortable positions, either squashed up in a bed with us all crammed in together or in some heap where Callie and I have tangled ourselves up.'

'Please,' she scoffs. 'He'd sleep with one of Lilah's nappies as a pillow if it meant you were within arm's reach. How is magic training going? I ask because your eyes are still a little bloodshot.'

'It's going well. Just building up my stamina again,' I tell her. 'Still waiting on my Sight to appear, but otherwise, everything else is back up and running.' I step over a fallen tree and help her across. 'It's weird to have the knowledge but not the strength or skill. But I'll get there. I just need to keep practising. I may have overdone it this morning with all the whooshing.'

'Callie does enjoy a good whoosh,' Amara laughs.

The two children follow the rugged path deeper into the woods, towards the sound of a gently flowing river.

As we arrive in the clearing, I hear a booming laugh.

'There's my beautiful granddaughter! Come here, you!'

Callie sprints towards Dad as he stands at the edge of the river and throws herself into his waiting arms.

Dad encases her in a bear hug, kissing her cheek over and over, making her laugh as his beard tickles her skin.

His long grey hair is tied back in a ponytail, as ever. And he still insists on wearing those hideous flannel shirts every day.

'Did you bring your fishing rods?' he asks both Callie and Finley.

'We did,' they both declare, waving around their sticks like lunatics.

'Good stuff. You know what to do. Off you go.'

He lowers Callie to the ground, and she joins Finley by the bucket. The two start wrapping wire around their sticks.

Dad's eyes land on me and I let out the most relieved sigh. Amara lets my hand go and lingers back a little as I go to meet him.

I get much the same as Callie did. An enormous embrace and several kisses on the cheek.

'Good morning, Buttons,' he says, still holding me tight.

'Morning, Dad.'

'I'm so glad to see you.'

'You saw me last night at dinner.'

'And I was glad to see you then, too.'

To be in his arms is to be encased by a forcefield of protection. He's my Dad. And I still thank the universe that I get this chance to be his daughter again.

I fight the urge to burst into tears as I get bombarded with images of him strapped to that table, slowly being carved up. My grip gets tighter, and I feel hot tears spring into my eyes. He winces and I know I've accidentally shared with him a glimpse of that misery through my Mental magic.

'I'm sorry,' I whimper, pulling back. 'I didn't mean-'

'It's okay,' he calms, refusing to let me go. 'Don't pull away for me. I don't even remember that. Gabriel had me tucked far away as that happened. This memory is yours, and I'll share in it with you so you don't face it alone. I'm here. It's okay.'

He lets me grip him in my vice-like hold.

'It's okay, Buttons. Deep breaths. Where are you?'

'I'm here,' I reply with a calming breath. 'With you.'

'And what are you?'

I swallow down the sob attempting to claw its way up my throat.

'I'm safe. We're all safe.'

'That's my girl.'

He doesn't release me. He doesn't ease up. He never does. If I don't let go first, I'm sure we would start sprouting roots.

I step back, but he keeps a hold of my hand and a comforting smile firmly in place.

'Another bad night? You look tired.'

'It was just a nightmare,' I tell him.

'Gabriel said it put a crack in the ceiling,' Amara adds. When I glare over my shoulder at her, she shrugs. 'What? It did!'

I look back to Dad with an eye roll. 'It didn't bring the house down or start a fire, though. I choose to look on the bright side of things.'

'That's my girl,' Dad chuckles. 'If you want to catch up on some sleep, you can lie down there if you like?' He gestures to the selection of blankets and cushions he has laid out for us all. 'Catch up on some rest whilst the kids and I catch dinner.'

'I want to watch,' I insist, glancing at Callie as she frowns with frustration at the knotted mess of wire at the end of her stick. Finley has made his already and is quick to help her sort out her chaos. 'I like watching you guys.'

'You're free to join us if you like. I brought an extra line.'

'I'm good. You do the grandpa thing. I'll do the tired mum thing.'

'Oh!' Amara says happily, raising her hand. 'I'll be doing that too.' She makes for the blanket.

'You will come back to the house after, right? Cook whatever it is you catch?' I ask almost pleadingly.

'Of course, sweetheart. I'd love to.'

'Have you spoken to the Council lately?' I ask.

'I may have.' He narrows his eyes, waiting to see if I know what he knows.

'I went to see The Stolen this morning about the missing people,' I tell him. He slumps in relief that I'm in the know and that he doesn't have to tip toe around it.

'Are they involved?'

'No. It's not them. They have some missing people too. And one of the girls mentioned mutilated animals. I left Gabriel and Collins at the village to investigate a bit more.'

'How was the visit to that hovel?'

'Oh, you know. Same old. They called me every name under the sun and spat at us. But I did save a baby and more of them came back to the village with us.' I fill with pride. 'The looks on their faces when the others all rushed over to help them was something else.'

'The rest will come around eventually. No one can live like that forever.'

'Some of them, maybe. But those leaders, the ones with those massive crucifixes around their necks... I'm not so sure about. They throw their religious beliefs around to the detriment of other people's lives. A baby would have died if I hadn't gone there today. Several kids came back with us, so that's something. But there are more. I don't like leaving them there.'

'You want me to pop over to the village after we're done here? See if I can do anything to help?'

'See if Clara is still there, more like.'

'No... that's not what I mean...' he stutters. 'She was there this morning, was she?'

'She was. She came to the cottage this morning to fetch us. She asked about you.'

'She did?'

I nod. 'You can ask her to join us for dinner if you want to.'

I wait. Sure enough, his cheeks begin to blush.

'I told you before. Ain't nothing going on with Clara and me. We're friends.'

'I think she would like to be a little more than friends, Dad. And it's obvious you do too.'

He grumbles and continues to redden.

I've watched them for months now. Going for their walks. Meeting up for lunches. They seem to have gotten relatively close whilst I was "*away*".

Dad insists there is nothing more than friendship between them. But I know that there's a ton more and then some.

'Invite her,' I attempt again.

'Maybe another time. Besides, she'll probably bring Ash with her.'

'And?'

Dad sort of grimaces and shrugs.

'Ash unsettles me a little. It's his eyes. They're... kinda...'

'Familiar, right?' I agree, glad I'm not the only one. 'In a really eerie way. They look at you and it feels like they look straight through you.'

'Exactly.'

'Well, I'm supposed to be going around theirs for dinner at some point. He keeps going on about his girlfriend being desperate to meet me.'

'Maybe she wants your autograph?' Dad teases.

'Grandpa, we're ready!' Callie declares in her usual little sing-song voice.

'Yes, ma'am,' he grins. 'Duty calls.'

He turns away and joins the children.

I join Amara on the blanket and watch the three wade into the river. They cast their line and set to work, listening

to Dad's instructions with intense concentration, determined to learn all there is to learn about catching fish for
no other reason than to be the first one to catch the biggest.

*The rope pinches the skin around my wrists and my
screams get stuck in my throat, refusing to come out, the
way they always do in a dream.*

*I pull and I pull, desperate to stop the horrific acts of
violence playing out before me.*

To stop Gabriel's murder.

Grayson is carving out his eyes and spitting in his face.

*Behind me, Theo laughs. He laughs as he picks up Callie's
limp body and starts walking away with her.*

No. No. No... NO!

I sit with such speed, the world spins. Finally, the scream
finds its freedom and tears itself from my throat, exploding
into the air like a shriek direct from hell.

My magic surges. The ground trembles beneath me and
a deafening rushing sound pierces the air.

That, and screams.

Tears blur my vision and all I see are shapes scrambling
about as the others yell and shout.

'LILLY! LILLY, STOP!' Dad bellows, his voice filled with
panic and fear. 'WAKE UP!'

I blink, clearing my vision.

Dad has Finley and Callie under his arms and is frantically running towards us, his eyes firmly on the sky above
him.

The kids are screaming and coughing up water. They're all soaked through.

Amara is holding the baby, yelling at them all to run!

RUN!

It hits me suddenly that the river... it's gone!

I look up.

'Fuck...' I hiss.

In my sleep, the horror of my dreams manifested in my power, and has spilled out.

The water is overhead, suspended in the air, swirling like it's a raging sea in the middle of a violent storm.

Amongst it are boulders and rocks.

And it's starting to fall. The whole damn lot.

I look at Dad and the children in his arms.

They're not going to make it.

I get to my feet, but before I've even stood, I send myself straight to them and raise my hands up high, keeping the ceiling of water and stone from crashing down on top of them.

The weight of it forces me into the silt and mud as deep as my knees.

"RUN!' I scream at them.

Dad hasn't even stopped.

But the weight is too much, and my stamina just isn't there.

The rocks start to fall first, slamming to the ground with heavy thuds. Dad dodges them, leaping left to right as the kids keep screaming. Amara stretches out her hand, using her magic to redirect them away.

Then the water starts to slip, falling like a light rain at first, and then a downpour.

I can't hold it. None of it.

I look at Dad and the kids. I look at Amara.

And I divert my power to them instead.

They all turn and face me.

I send them home in a forceful "whoosh". Back to the cottage, far from me and my inability to fucking control myself.

Back to safety.

I close my eyes and take a deep breath just as the water crashes down on top of me, swallowing me whole.

Chapter 6

I claw at the water, reaching for the surface with desperation. My legs are still buried deep in the mud, holding me down, keeping me a prisoner under the churning water.

I call my magic, but all I get is a headache.

Headache or not, if I do nothing, I'll drown. And I did not fight all I have fought to die because of my own fucking stupidity!

I reach down and sink my hands in the silt, and with my final breath, I scream in the effort. The ground erupts below my feet and sets me free. The water becomes clouded with the dirt and mud as I kick against the water still swirling around me, churning and rolling me in every possible direction.

I finally break the surface.

Greedily, I take in breath after breath as I tread the turbulent water, waiting for it to calm. The odd splash happens as rocks and debris return to earth.

It's a damn good job Mama Quinn taught me to swim during those five years we lived together in the human world, hiding from those who still hunted us.

Shame I can't teach myself any fucking control.

I swim to shore and wade out, falling on the grass and coughing against the water and thick blood sliding down my throat. It drips from my nose and my head pounds in my skull.

I sit to try and catch my breath. I've over-exerted. That's a dangerous thing to do, especially for me with so much access to the magic of the Arcane Realm.

Shivering all over, I pull my knees close to my chest and rest my chin on top of them, watching as the water continues to calm and return to its usual state. It's less than a minute before everything looks as it was, like nothing even happened.

Something warm trickles down the side of my face. Reaching up, I see blood on the tips of my fingers, and I wince at the sharp pain from beyond my hairline.

I must have taken a knock somewhere along the line.

I'm okay. It will heal soon enough.

Who am I kidding?

I'm far from fucking okay.

With a sniff, I wipe the tear that slides down my cheek and grind my teeth together, loathing myself completely.

I'm a liability. A risk.

A stupid nightmare could have seriously hurt the children and my dad. I ball up my fists and slam them into the ground. It cracks beneath me as my Physical magic spikes, making me ten times stronger than I should be.

Another stabbing pain ripples through my skull as my body protests against the magic.

I can't let this happen again. I need to get this shit under control.

There must be something I can do. A spell to stop the nightmares. Perhaps I can do to myself what I did to others with the Branding spell and hide all those memories.

But remembering all the suffering is how I know it will never happen again. If I get rid of it, I may forget why it is so important to keep fighting for what's right.

Either way, until I figure out a way to stop the nightmares, I know that there is something I *can* do to stop my magic from spiking whilst I sleep.

I grab the sleeve of my top and tug, tearing it free. I search the debris of the woodland floor and find some dried-up old vines. Using a jagged rock, I slice open my hand and soak the vine in the pooling blood. Then I weave it through the fabric of my torn-up shirt.

Ten minutes or so pass. And I hold in my hand a very makeshift binding spell.

It's temporary, I tell myself. *Just temporary. And only for when I sleep.*

I slide it into my pocket and slump.

I hope that the others are okay and not too pissed off with me.

From behind me, there's a horrendous screech. It's one full of pain. It resonates through the entire woodland.

All around me, the wildlife explodes into life.

And not in a good way.

They're fleeing, taking to the skies, or scrabbling away into the brush.

The cry doesn't sound human. I think it's an animal or something.

It cries out again, and there's something about it that makes me run ice-cold to my very core.

It's an unearthly scream. One that feels all kinds of wrong. Going against nature and twisting it into something broken.

Every part of my being says run. The hairs on the back of my neck stand on end and I feel a sudden pit of despair swell in my belly.

I get to my feet, ready to run away just like every other creature here.

But my heart tells me otherwise, and instead, I run as fast as I can towards it.

The cry continues as I hurtle deeper into the woods, running over the fallen logs and branches, past the gnarly trees and protruding boulders.

I emerge in a small clearing, darkened by the shade of the canopy of leaves above. I know these woods pretty well but have never seen this clearing before.

It's like something from a fairy tale. Pristine white flowers bloom all over the place. A rock formation covered in moss mimics that of a beautiful woman sleeping half in the ground. Vines sway in the gentle breeze, and the smell of lavender and lilies fills the air.

In the very centre is a creature struggling for its life. The same creature I had heard rumours of existing in whispers and songs. But never actually seen.

'A unicorn...' I stand, mesmerised by the mythical creature of pure white with a silver horn protruding from its forehead.

Its hooves have been bound together with wire and it thrashes on the floor, trapped on its side.

It takes me a moment to realise that she's not alone.

A cloaked figure stands over her, their face obscured by a black hood. They're tall, but other than that, I can see no other discerning features.

They don't see me standing in the treeline. As I step closer, the figure kneels beside her and pulls out a weapon. A long blade that curves.

A scythe.

Before I can react, the cloaked figure buries the scythe into her belly and draws it upwards in a swift, violent, and unhesitant motion.

The scream the unicorn makes... my god. I go dizzy as its pain and terror seep into the air.

The cloaked figure thrusts their hand deep into her belly, making her cry out even more.

They pull something out of her. Something small, too soaked with blood to truly see what the hell it is.

The hooded figure lifts their gaze.

They look right at me.

They drop the scythe, choosing to surrender their weapon rather than release whatever organ they stole from the still writhing beast.

But when they thrust out their hand, I realise they have no need for a bladed weapon.

Deep blue lightning springs to life from their fingers and a stream of it shoots at me.

I raise my hand and send my own Energy magic back. The red of my lightning clashes with the blue of theirs and sends violent sparks in all directions, hitting the ground and scorching the earth or splintering the bark of the tree trunks surrounding us.

My power is still in its infancy. I have only had this magic since I first arrived. This person has clearly had it much longer. Probably since the first day they arrived here five years ago. I feel its strength. I sense the control they wield over it. I may not have the stamina they have, and the pressure in my head is unbearable already, but I have other realms of power.

I reach out and create my fire with my free hand. It spills to the ground and forms one of my fire wolves. The flaming creature springs into action, its teeth bared and lava-like saliva spilling from its lips. It growls and roars as it goes for the kill, its vibrant red flaming paws scorching the ground on contact.

The cloaked figure waves their hand and breaks our lightning connection before reaching into their pocket and retrieving some kind of small vial. They throw it at my wolf's feet and I yell as it explodes in a blast of black smoke. The smoke seems to roar as it weaves itself around my wolf, smothering it. Suffocating it. My wolf howls as it struggles against the shadow. It thrashes and falls to the ground, and within seconds, both the smoke and the wolf are gone.

I turn to the hooded figure, just in time to see them toss a dagger at me. I throw myself out of the way, but not quickly enough. It scratches my cheek, the tip of the blade drawing blood before I land on the ground.

The figure runs towards me, lightning crawling over one hand and the deep red blood from the unicorn dripping over whatever the hell they stole from its body in the other.

I expel a blast of Telekinetic power and the unknown assailant is sent soaring back, hurtling through the brush and out of sight.

The dying creature looks at me, panic spilling out of its beautiful eyes.

It continues to buck and struggle. Each movement it makes causes more blood to spill from the gaping wound in its belly.

I run to it.

'I can help you!' I insist, struggling to get past its flailing body. 'I can fix you!'

It stills, looking into my eyes, and I know it understood me.

I drop to my knees and rest my hands over the slash before channelling my Physical magic into her.

I pant, looking anxiously beyond the thick brush, watching for the attacker to return.

Her blood seeps through my fingers and into the ground. As soon as it does, all that was alive starts to die. The grass turns black. The flowers rot. The vines decay. The moss-covered woman cracks and crumbles into dust.

The unicorn's eyes are on me completely. I can feel her fear and pain as if it were my own. I feel her misery. Her grief.

I start to cry for her.

'Hold on,' I tell her. 'Just hold on.'

The cut starts to close. The blood slowly stops.

But my own starts to fall, sliding from my nose and ears.

'A little more...' I whisper, forcing myself on. 'A little... more...'

But the creature... she lets out her last breath.

Just as the last flower dies, so too does the unicorn.

All that surrounds me now is death. The woodland is decayed, and the unicorn is still.

Gone.

Murdered.

I lift my head and look into the woods where I sent the monster who did this. I hear no attempt for his return. No rustling of leaves or snapping of twigs. No crackle from his lightning or the singing of steel.

I take another look at the unfortunate creature, her lifeless eyes still trained on me and the remnants of her emotions still in my soul.

And before I can think it through, I go after the fucker.

Again, I'm running through the woods. My hands and my clothes are stained red. Hot tears sting my eyes and dark wrath is coursing through me.

'GET BACK HERE!' I bellow. 'YOU GET THE FUCK BACK HERE!'

I run faster and harder, but there's no sign of anyone else. No tracks. No pathways. Nothing.

When a twig snaps to my left, I spin and raise my hand. My red fire springs to life on my fingers.

I'm ready for some payback.

'Easy! It's me! It's me, Buttons!'

Dad swiftly dismounts his horse, panting and sweating from his hasty ride back from the cottage. He looks me up and down.

'What the hell happened to you?' He rushes over, looking at the copious amounts of blood drenching my already soaked clothes. 'You're hurt! Fuck!'

'That's not my blood,' I tell him, still looking around us.

'But this is!' He gestures to the cut on my cheek and the damage caused by the falling rocks at the lake. He touches the blood beneath my nose and sees it at my ears. 'You've used too much magic. What the hell happened here?'

'There was... a man. I think it was a man. He attacked me. He...' I continue looking around us, hoping to see a glimpse of the killer.

But whoever it was, they've gone.

Dad takes my face in his hands.

'What happened here, Buttons?' he asks. 'Whose blood are you soaked in if not your own?'

'Is everyone okay? Callie... Amara and her kids-'

'You sent us all back to the cottage. Everyone is absolutely fine. No one got so much as a scratch. Everyone is just worried about you. Now, tell me what the fuck happened!'

I take his hands in mine.

'Follow me. I'll show you.'

Chapter 7

D ad stands over the dead unicorn with his hands atop his head, lost in bewilderment and shock at the butchery before him.

'I just...' He lets out a long breath and shakes his head, glancing at the death of the woodland around us and the unicorn. 'I can't understand this. Why the hell would someone want to murder a unicorn? How could they even find one?'

'What do you mean, find one? It's in the middle of the woods.'

'They're hidden creatures, Buttons. That's what Connor Quinn says, anyway. I should know. The kid's been trying to find one since we got here. That and a sodding dragon. He says they cloak themselves from view, which is why it's so rare to see them. You only see them if they want to be seen.'

'That would explain why I had never seen this clearing before today.'

'Precisely. I'm pretty sure this is its nest.' He looks sadly at the rotten space that now surrounds us. 'Or it was. I can't understand how someone who meant to harm it could find it.'

'I tried to save her.' I crouch down beside her body, resting my hand on her back. 'I sealed the wound with my magic, but she died anyway. I don't think I was strong enough.'

Dad crouches beside me and rests his hand beside mine.

'I found her because I think she was calling for help. It was the strangest thing. I felt like I knew what she was feeling. That she was communicating. She was so afraid. She was so heartbroken.'

'She called, you came, and you did everything you could,' he comforts. 'You can't blame yourself for this.'

'I should have healed her faster. I would have if that bastard didn't attack me. If I was stronger. If I had practised more and built up my stamina.'

'You have been pushing yourself every day. You're doing all you can-'

'We need to find out who is responsible. It can't go un-punished! First the missing witches. Now this?'

'We will, Buttons.' His hand rests on mine. 'I promise you. We will. But first, let's get you back home. Callie is a little spooked, and you need to be there for her. Besides, if there is someone powerful and stupid enough to try and kill you, I don't want you out here anymore. Not this exhausted.'

'I'm not scared of whoever did this, Dad. I can deal with them.'

'You're a baby witch. You've only had your magic for a few months. Others here have been training since the day they arrived.'

'I'm perfectly capable,' I snap. 'And I'm not a baby witch.'

'Either way, you need to go home. Your daughter needs you alive, Lilly. We need you safe and right now...' He looks around us. 'You're not safe.'

'Is she scared of me?' I ask. 'Callie?'

'No. Just worried and wanting her mum.' He stands and holds out his hand. 'Let's give her what she wants, hmm?'

'What about the unicorn? We can't just leave her here like this.'

'I'll talk to Gabriel when he returns. We'll figure it out.' He flexes his fingers. 'You let us worry about this. You focus on Callie and yourself for now. Please. I just want to get you back to safety.'

I take his hand and he pulls me to my feet.

With a final glance at the dull and lifeless eyes of the most magical of creatures, we head towards his horse, mount up, and start the ride home.

Chapter 8

The last thing I want is for Callie to see her mother smothered in blood, especially after scaring the hell out of her at the lake. So Dad goes in first and distracts her as I sneak upstairs to the bathroom.

I strip off and step into the shower to clean myself off, scrubbing the blood from my skin with soap that smells of lavender. A smell I now recoil from as it's the scent that filled my nostrils as the poor creature bled to death.

I shut the shower off and get dressed, the whole time, replaying the incident over and over.

Who the fuck was in that cloak and what did they take from the unicorn?

And why?

Is it connected to the missing witches? Are they lying in the woods somewhere, carved up and left to rot?

The girl from The Stolen's camp did say that animals had been mutilated a few miles away.

This all seems far too connected.

I shudder at the memory of that lightning. Not the lightning today from the stranger, but Theo's and Grayson's lightning. Their sneers. Their hands...

They're dead, I remind myself. As I do every day, again and again.

They. Are. Dead.

Energy magic is one of the seven realms, and despite all the positives that realm has, it's feared and considered a little darker and more dangerous than the rest, all because it belonged to Theo and Grayson.

It's just an unfortunate coincidence that the first person to attack me since arriving here would have that power to wield against me.

They also had that powder that created the black smoke. It was a spell. A potion of some kind. The teachings of spells and potions are limited and only taught in controlled spaces and to those who have been vetted. We're all so new at this and magic is dangerous. Spells and potions... that's highly restricted.

Someone must have a list of names of those who have been learning this stuff.

Someone must know something about all of this!

The mirror on the wall cracks as I furiously wrap myself in a towel. That's not good. Closing my eyes. I take a very forced, calming breath. I can't allow my anger to get the better of me. I can't!

When I open the bathroom door, I find Callie sitting on the floor with her legs crossed, brushing the hair on her favourite doll.

She looks up and shows me a beautiful smile.

'Hi, Mummy,' she greets. 'Are you feeling better?'

Callie peers around the side of the door and frowns. I look back and see my bloody clothes left on the bathroom floor. I quickly step out and close the door before kneeling in front of her, worried I've traumatised the poor child even further.

'Hi, sweet girl. I'm perfectly fine. Are you okay?' I sweep her hair from her face. Such a mess of deep brown curls, the exact same shade as Gabriel's.

Her eyes narrow as she reaches out and runs her finger across my cheek. I wince.

'You got a cut,' she says quietly.

'Well,' I smile. 'That's an easy fix.' I rest my finger on the cut. My head hurts as I heal myself but to ease her worry, it's a small price to pay. 'Now tell me, are you okay? I know what happened must have scared you and I'm so sorry. I didn't mean to do that. Grandpa said you didn't get any scrapes or bruises.'

'Can you teach me to do that one day?' she asks. Her arms raise above her head as she makes an exaggerated *SWISSSHHH*. 'It was so cool. I wish I could do that.'

'One day you will,' I tell her. She scrambles into my lap and looks up at me with wonderous and curious eyes. 'That, and so much more. You know why?'

'Because I'm an Arcane Witch? Just like you?'

'That's right. And you know what else? I bet you'll be much better at it than me.'

'You really think so?'

'I know so.'

'When my magic comes, will I have nightmares like you do?' she asks, a tinge of concern tainting her words.

'No, baby,' I assure her. 'Mummy has bad dreams because she got very lost and because she had to fight the baddies we talked about. The baddies that wanted to stop us from using magic. Daddy and I told you about the baddies, remember?'

She nods, no doubt recalling the very light version of events that we described to her several months ago. That there were evil people who wanted to stop witches and put them in prison. A simple and lighter version of the truth, but a version, nonetheless. She knows that I was lost in another place, one that kept us apart for those first five years. And that sometimes, I have bad dreams about that place.

'You will never have to fight those baddies like we did because we beat them and now we're all safe,' I promise.

Images of the unicorn flash in my mind and I pull her closer.

'We're safe,' she repeats with a firm nod, tightening my arms around her middle. 'We're safe. We're here. And we're together. Right, Mummy?'

'Abosfudginglutely,' I agree, kissing her cheek. 'And I promise I'll make sure we stay that way. No matter what.'

Chapter 9

In the garden, between the cottage and the edge of the cliffs and close to the permanent Christmas tree, we have a campfire area set up. Logs act as benches and encircle a fire pit.

I watch Dad hold out his hand and expel a small flame into the fire pit. He's a natural at using it.

Well, he has had five years of practice, I remind myself.

As has everyone else, apparently.

I'm still enthralled by their use of magic. Seeing them all use it so openly and freely, I could watch it all day long.

We were supposed to have fish for dinner.

That didn't quite go according to plan. So instead, Amara made a ton of sandwiches.

We've all gathered at the fire's side. The children have wrapped themselves in blankets and are sitting with Amara, who has started reading them a story.

I take a short walk to the cliff's edge and steal a moment of solitude to look at the sea below. In the distance, a bob of seals breaks the water's surface. Birds do their final dives, and the sun is starting to sink into the horizon.

I glance back at my family. Amara reaches out her hand and calls a blanket into her outstretched fingers before using her magic to remove a spider Finley has caught and is about to show Callie in the hopes of a scream.

Smiling, I wrap my blanket tighter around my shoulders and return my gaze to the sea.

'It's one hell of a view,' Dad says as he stands at my side.

'It sure is,' I reply with a sigh, my mind on a million other things than the view.

The sun reflects in his eyes before they land on me.

'You feeling okay, Buttons?' he asks. 'How's your head?'

'It will be fine after some rest. My head is the least of my worries. Callie should never see me like that,' I shake my head in self-disgust. 'She waited five years for me. She was told stories about her mother. A great witch. A brave witch. One of strength and heart.' I look at him. 'It's all a bunch of bullshit though. I mean, look at what she's got. A mother who barely sleeps. One who wakes up screaming and almost drowns her. Who comes home covered in blood.'

'She has a mother who loves her more than anything. A mother she loves just as much. A mother who is all those things and so much more. Not that Callie would even care about your powers or deeds. She loves you because you are her mum. A damn good mum, might I add.'

'I could have killed her today,' I admit painfully.

'No. You couldn't, and you wouldn't. You got everyone out of the way and risked your own safety doing so. It wasn't your fault what happened at the lake today. You've been through hell, Buttons. People don't just get over the darkness you've suffered.'

'You guys seem to be getting on with life okay.'

'Because we've had five years of living here and settling into a well-earned peace. You had to survive another five years of misery after everything you went through. Five years on the run without your family and your magic.'

'I just wish I could be like you guys. Like Gabriel.'

'You know, Gabriel was a real mess when we arrived. And I mean, a real fucking mess. The man locked himself away in his room every single night and sobbed. We would hear him sometimes, utterly raging at the world. Hurling threats and insults at the air, hating that you were lost to him. Lost to Callie. Sometimes, he would disappear for days. When we found him, he'd be passed out from booze at some location that meant something to you both. The Bloodstone locations. The land where The Orchard was to be built. In London, where The British Museum stood. I've never seen such a broken man.'

'Really?' I ask, feeling a lump form in my throat at the idea of him so lost.

'Callie would cry and she would cry. There was just no comforting her.' He shows me a sad smile. 'But every time we tracked him down, he would get on his feet, take a deep breath and be there. When she was in his arms, she never cried. And when he was with her, he could live a little easier. They needed each other to survive, so they clung to each other. They saved each other. And now they will do the same for you, and you for them.' He peers back at Callie as she waves at us.

'I'm so scared of her getting hurt. The idea of anything bad happening to her is enough to drive me insane.'

'No one would be foolish enough to come after her. Not with you and the rest of us here. Even the idiot today ran when he realised who you were.'

'It's not that,' I whisper. 'It's not other people hurting her
I'm scared of. I know that no child is more protected than
her. It's me. What if I go dark again?'

'You're not going anywhere and even if you did, which
you won't, I would never let any harm come to her.'

'I was her age when Mum tried to drown me in Uncle
Harry's bathtub,' I remind him. 'I was her age when I became his prisoner. When I was first locked in that attic,
it wasn't long after that when the beatings started. The
hunger. The humiliation. Ryan-'

'Don't. Don't speak that filthy name to me. Never mention that house again.' His lip trembles as he violently
shakes his head. 'Please. Don't.'

'My point is... you said the same thing, I'm sure. You
looked at me when I was that small, that innocent, and
vowed no harm would ever befall me. And I'm certain
that you meant it when you said it. But it did. I suffered,
Dad. Things happened beyond your control, and I *really*
suffered. What if she suffers too? If I go dark again, there's
no one strong enough to stop a Broken Arcane.'

'Yes there is. There's you. You defeated her once, and if
you must, you will defeat her again. And even Broken, your
Broken side protected her. To the detriment of the entire
world, might I add, but she did. Callie also has Gabriel as
her father, and he would never let any harm come to either
of you. And she has Amara, Collins, The Quinns, Bias...
wherever he is these days. And she has me. I wish you had
as much faith in yourself as we all have in you. You defeated
your Broken self, along with the rest of the humans. You.
You literally saved the world, Buttons.' He rests his hand

firmly on my shoulder. 'Now it's time for you to be brave enough to live in it.'

With another glance at the others by the fire, I nod.

'You're right,' I tell him. 'You're absofuckinglutely right.'

'Come on,' he says, taking my hand. 'Let's eat.'

Gabriel and Collins are yet to return. Callie and Finley struggle to stay awake with their full bellies and the warmth of the fire, and I can't engage in any conversation at all. I'm far too distracted. As Amara tries to talk to me in a hushed whisper about what happened with the unicorn, I hardly hear her. I'm too busy asking my own questions over and over in my head.

'I think it's time we put these two to bed,' Dad declares, getting to his feet and looking at the two children falling asleep side by side. 'What do you think?'

I nod, and he reaches out, taking Callie in one arm and Finley in his other. They both slump into him as he stands.

'Can you stay at mine tonight,' I ask both Amara and Dad. 'The kids can sleep in Callie's room and you can each take one of the guest rooms. If that's alright with you guys?'

'Better than all right,' Amara nods.

But Dad looks on suspiciously.

'Why?' he asks.

'I just need to do something. Can you watch Callie? Please?' I interrupt as he goes to argue. 'I'll be back in an hour or so. I won't get any rest until I do this.'

'Do what?' Amara urges, getting to her feet.

'I just want to check something. It won't be dangerous. I promise.'

'Gabriel will be back soon. Wait for him.'

'I can manage. I'll be right back.' I look at Callie sleeping soundly in his arms. 'Watch my daughter for me, Dad. Keep her safe.'

With a swirl of dirt and wind, I fade from their sight.

Chapter 10

I stand across the dirt road, looking at the stone cottage perched at the side of the riverbank. The water wheel continuously turns and fireflies hover above the water's surface. The smell of freshly baked pie wafts from the open window and the sound of music accompanies it.

I smile, hearing the Irish jig playing on a music box made using a set of pins placed on a revolving disc plugging at the tuned teeth.

Lois always loved her music. She always had her music, no matter where we were or what was happening around us.

I walk towards the door and give a gentle knock.

It soon opens, and one of my favourite people answers.

'My dear girl!'

'Good evening, Mama Quinn.' I grin, thrilled to see her.

Almost as thrilled as she is to see me because I'm soon wrapped in an enormous hug and hauled inside.

'Oh, it's so good to see you,' she says, still embracing me tightly. 'So bloody good!'

'I saw you last week,' I chuckle.

'Far too long. Come!' she insists, guiding me inside. 'I just made some apple and red berry pie. Sit. Have some with us.'

As I turn into the lounge, I meet with Papa Quinn.

'There's my favourite Arcane Witch,' he smiles.

'How are you doing?' I ask, reaching up and throwing my arms around his neck.

'Better for seeing you.' He quickly guides me inside and before I've had the chance to sit, I have a plate of pie in one hand and a glass of whiskey in the other.

I politely refuse the whiskey, but I sure as shit will have some of that pie. Mama Quinn's pie... it's the best!

'Is everything okay?' Papa Quinn asks. 'It's not like you to be out late.'

'Or alone,' Mama adds.

Her usual *no-bullshit-here* trait is still firmly in place.

That woman has seen me in the very depths of misery, anger and despair. We survived half a decade on the run together.

She's more of a mother to me than anyone else in my whole life.

'I need to talk to Connor. Is he home?' I ask.

'No, he's not, I'm afraid,' she says. 'He's gone down to that sodding cove again.'

'Oh. When will he be back?'

'He left a couple of days ago. He said he'll be gone a while.' She offers an unbothered shrug. 'He could turn up any time.'

My stomach drops.

'Y-you've not spoken to him for a few days?' I ask.

'No. Connor has been exploring this new realm relentlessly, obsessed with the creatures that live here. He's convinced there's a dragon down at that cove,' she tells me.

Her eyes narrow as she sees the blood drain from my face. 'What's happened?'

'The cove. How far to ride to it?'

'A few hours. Maybe more.' She furrows her brow further and shifts to the edge of the sofa. 'Why?'

'I need to ask him something. About unicorns.'

'Unicorns?' they both ask together.

'Hmmm. Does he keep notes or anything about the creatures he researches?'

'In his room. There are dozens of books filled with his findings. Good luck trying to find anything specific. Connor is thorough, but he's not organised,' she says with an eye roll. 'He's the most unorganised and messy boy I have ever known.'

I can't help but smirk. Her entire house is littered with books and notes. They pile up around doors and overflow on the tables and chairs.

The Quinns love to learn. And this is a whole new world full of the unknown.

'To be honest with you,' she adds. 'He's not found much out about unicorns. He's too busy obsessing over dragons.'

I chew on my lower lip.

'Oh no. I know that look,' Mama Quinn groans.

'Can you show me on a map where the Cove is?' I ask.

Papa Quinn has already darted into action, pulling out a map from an over-filled drawer packed to the brim with sheets detailing the landscape. He places it in my hand and points to a section on the map.

'This is where we are here.' He trails his finger upwards. 'Connor should be here, camped at the base of these cliffs.

This path here is the best one to take. If you leave in the morning, you should get there by-'

'What direction is this cliff, here?' I ask, pointing at the edge of the landmass closest to where their cottage stands.

'That direction,' he tells me, pointing out of the kitchen window. 'It's a thirty-minute walk.'

'How far up the coast can you see from there?'

'Several miles.' He taps a protruding part of the land on the map. 'From the beach, you can see to here.'

'And from there, where can you see too?' I ask.

He replies with a quizzical frown but draws his finger along to the next protruding land mass.

'You can see to here.'

'And then?'

'What are you planning?' Mama Quinn asks.

'I can't yet send myself to places I haven't seen. But if I see it, I can get to it.'

'So, you plan to magically leapfrog your way along the coastline until you get to Connor?'

'Pretty much,' I shrug, looking at the map. 'So, after this one here?'

He looks to his wife anxiously, seeking out permission to spill the beans.

'Well, you might as well tell her. If she wants to go, she's gonna go.' Mama Quinn rummages for a quill and dips it in some ink before sitting beside me and marking out locations.

'Can this not wait until morning?' she asks as I get to my feet.

'Maybe. But then I'll be awake all night worrying.'

'About what?' she asks.

'Hopefully, nothing. Don't worry, Mama Quinn.' I embrace her again. 'Can I take some more pie? Connor will sulk if he knows I didn't bring any.'

'Sure thing. You want me to come to the cove with you? I can. It's no bother.'

'No need. I'm perfectly safe on my own.'

'More like you're worried and would rather only put yourself in harm's way,' she mutters before pulling back to look me in the eye. 'Plus, you look spent, Lilly. Have you been overdoing the magic again?'

The woman knows me well.

'I have to go. I don't want you to worry, but there have been a few disappearances in the village. Witches who haven't been seen or heard from in a few days.'

She gasps. 'Is it those idiots? The Stolen fools in the woods?'

'No. I went there today. It's not them.'

'Why do you need to talk to Connor?'

'There was an incident with a unicorn, and I'd like his opinion. Plus... if you haven't seen him for a few days, I would feel much better making sure he's alright.

'You don't think Connor's missing, do you?' she asks, the blood draining from her face as she clutches her heart. 'I want to come.'

'I'll return as soon as I can and let you know what I find,' I assure her.

'And, what does this all have to do with unicorns?' asks Papa Quinn.

'One was killed,' I tell them. 'By a man. I think he was a man. He had a hood. And a knife. He cut open the creature and took something from her.'

The look of horror on both their faces is enough to make me shudder.

'I'm definitely coming with you to find Connor.' Mama Quinn starts gathering her belongings.

'I can't take you,' I say apologetically. 'You're right. I'm at my limit with my magic at the moment. My head is pounding and taking people with me adds more strain. It will be hard work to get myself to Connor. I can't load myself up even more by taking you.'

'But... what if he's hurt?'

'Then I'll bring him straight home. If he's not there, I'll return as quickly as possible to tell you.'

'So, if we don't see you, that's a good thing?' Papa Quinn asks, tilting his head to the side and rubbing the back of his neck.

'Yes. That means I've found him and we're talking about the unicorn.'

'Where is Gabriel?' Mama Quinn asks.

'At the village, looking for the missing people.'

'Is your father with Callie?' she asks.

I nod. 'Amara and the kids too.'

'Then I'll take them some pie,' she states, resuming her packing.

'You don't have to,' I try. Uselessly.

'Nonsense. In times of trouble, we are stronger and safer together. We're a family. That's how it works. Darling?'

She barely has to look at her husband for him to know she wants him to pack their bags. He leaves the room and rushes upstairs.

She rests her hands on my shoulders, a severe look of concern on her face.

'I know you would feel better having us over at yours to help look after Callie. Just in case. So that's where we will be. We will protect your family as you go and look for my boy.'

'Are you sure you don't mind?'

It's true. I would feel much better having everyone together.

'Any excuse to get some Callie time is good enough for me. Now, let me get you something.' She rushes off to the kitchen and I hear the odd clatter before she returns and offers me a glass of some green sludge. 'Drink this.'

'Erm... why?' I give it a sniff and recoil at the putrid smell burning my nostrils.

'It's a remedy I've been working on. It's all-natural. Seeing as I'm the only non-magical being here, I'm making a point of enhancing my knowledge of herbal remedies for magical ailments. This one is for magical fatigue. It will just give you a little boost. And an extra charge to the neurons and some added sugars that-'

'It will help my headache?'

'It will help your headache.'

That's all I need to hear. I down it, the slime and lumps making me gag.

'But you know that if you push too far too quick, you can seriously hurt yourself,' she adds. 'If you overwork a muscle, it can tear. It can become irreparably damaged. You must take it easy with your magic until your body can catch up with your ability.'

I groan and try not to vomit all over her carpet as I hand back the empty glass.

'I know,' I insist, swallowing hard. 'But there's someone out there hurting us. I can't sit about and do nothing. Gabriel and Collins are with the Council at the village. Bias has gone off again. And Connor could be in danger.'

'You could wait for Gabriel to return from the village.'

'He has things to deal with just as I do. Please, don't worry. I'll be fine. I know my limits.'

With their bags packed and their horses saddled, they insist first on taking me to the coast before they carry on to my cottage.

Papa Quinn shows me the first piece of land I will need to get myself to. It's still visible, but the sun is setting, so I'm unsure how much light I have left.

With a final hug, we say our goodbyes. He gives me a lantern to help light my way, and I fade from their sights before appearing on another section of beach, further up the coast.

I can't see them from this distance, but I know that Mama and Papa Quinn are still there.

I turn to find the next bit of land I need to get to, far off in the horizon.

'Okay, magic. Please don't give up on me now. Please... please just get me to Connor. Please let him be okay.'

Three hops later, I land on my knees, dizzy as fuck and with a headache so bad I wretch.

I still have one final jump to do, but first, I need to get to the right place so I can see where I need to go.

I start walking, climbing over the rocks protruding from the sand as I make my way around the jutting cliff face blocking my view of my next destination. The wind whips across my face and as the tide creeps in, so does the chill.

I stop as I round the cliffs and look ahead to what should be the final jump, barely visible in this light.

It's a high and brutally steep cliff's edge that juts out far into the darkening sea. The steep face is jagged and merciless, reaching high up and dropping sharply below. At the very top is where I need to go. So that is what I aim for.

I summon my magic and cast my spell, sending me to the top of the cliff.

My feet meet hard stone that crumbles loosely underfoot. The surface is barely any size at all. The cliff's drop is a few feet at my back and a few feet at my front.

'Shit,' I hiss, staggering as vertigo strikes.

I wasn't expecting such a narrow space for landing.

The wind is far fiercer up here than it was down on the beach, and I stumble a little against its force. The world spins as the use of my magic takes its toll. I lean over and heave, throwing up inches from my feet.

'Ow...' I groan, holding my head. 'Urgh... fuck me...'

I pull out the flask of water Lois packed in the bag with the pie and swill my mouth clean before having a look around.

Taking a few cautious steps forwards, I peer over the edge. Below is a secluded cove encasing a slight stretch of beach. It's hard to see much, but I see no sign of Connor or a camp at all.

Carefully, I walk along the rocks, further inland, where the pathway widens up. I follow a natural slope towards the cove, passing a blackberry bush and helping myself to a few to get rid of the horrendous taste in my mouth.

The path weaves into a narrow passage, and as I follow it, all I can think about is Connor in the grips of some lunatic with a knife.

Please don't let him be missing. Please... please let him be at the Cove, fanboying over dragons.

I can't stand the idea of returning home to tell Mama Quinn that her son is gone. That I have no idea where he is. That he could be dead.

My insides squirm at the mere idea of it.

There's a rustle of leaves. I stop, every sense heightened.

The rustling continues in the overgrowth to my left and gets closer.

It stops suddenly, and before I can call out to see who, or what, is there, there's a yell.

Someone tumbles from the top of the brush and lands at my feet with a painful groan. I pull my fist back, the tired and pathetic flicker of my fire barely alight in my skin.

They roll over and peer up at me.

'That looked like it hurt,' I laugh, extinguishing my fire.

'*Owwwwww*,' Connor groans, still on his back and his face scrunched up. He slowly opens his eyes and tilts his head in confusion. 'Lilly? What the hell are you doing here?'

I reach out and take his hand, wholly and utterly relieved to see him in one piece. Always a miracle, considering the sheer clumsiness of the guy.

'Looking for you. Where the hell did you just come from?' I peer up at the top of the bushes. 'You floating up there or something?'

'Cliff path suddenly ended,' he grumbles. 'It's so dark. I didn't see. Oh... *maaaaan!*' he whines, pulling out his satchel which oozes with berry juice. 'They're squashed to shit now.'

'Don't worry.' I hold up my own bag. 'Your mum sent pie.'

He happily takes it, opens it up and takes a big sniff.

Then he throws a cautious look at me.

'Why did she send you with pie?' He lowers the bag. 'What's happened?'

'Funny you should ask.' I rest my hands on his shoulders. 'Connor, what do you know about unicorns?'

'Huh?'

Chapter 11

Connor guides me back in the direction of his camp, leading us through the narrow pathways and steep recesses of the cliff's coastal paths.

His face is filled with disgust as I tell him what happened today. His mouth remains agape and a deep frown is etched on his brow as we walk.

I admit, retelling it brings bile to my throat.

Finally, we emerge on a flat bit of land, shielded from view by the thick overgrowth and jutting rocks from the high cliffs.

He's made it very homely, but then, he was a Nomad and spent many years of his life living on the road.

He has a sizeable canvas tent and a large canopy attached to protect himself from rain and sun. There's a little fold-out table holding stacks of books and a campfire burning with a black pot suspended over the flames. The smell of soup welcomes us. He has a couple of logs placed close to it with some blankets folded neatly on top.

He gestures to the logs.

'Sit,' he says, still in shock from my words. 'You look ready to drop. I'll... I'll get you some... erm... some food.'

He busies himself, ladling soup into a bowl, and then he joins me at the fire.

'Are you certain he took something from the unicorn?' he asks, spooning soup into his mouth but unable to focus on anything else but me.

'Positive.'

'And he took it from this part of her body?' he runs his finger along his side.

'If you were a unicorn, then yeah, that's where he took it from.'

'Well, that's not good,' he murmurs, looking deep into the flames. 'Not good at all.'

State the obvious.

'What do you know about unicorns?'

'Well, it's not so much what I know about unicorns as what I know about the dark transition of stealing magic from another creature through blood.' He swallows another mouthful and carries on. 'Take Vampires, for example. They existed by stealing energy, life, and blood from others. It turned them into blood-thirsty fuckers with little to no conscience or sense of humanity. It's unnatural and screws with the balance of nature. Of light and dark. And if someone is taking from a creature as pure and as light as a unicorn, that only makes it worse.' He lowers the bowl and rests his elbows on his knees. We both scoot closer to each other. 'If a witch is stealing from other magical creatures, then they are either making a potion or working up to performing a spell. Either way, whatever it is for, it's Dark Magic. Very dark.'

'But who? The only people around back when spells and potions were even a thing were Gabriel, Bias and Collins. And no one has been teaching Dark Magic.'

'Well, there was Rebecca,' he offers with a shrug.

'Rebecca Hooper died,' I remind him, as a sadness fills my chest. 'And there is no way she would have passed on anything dangerous to anyone else. Her most dangerous spells are in the journal, which I have safely hidden. Not that anyone could read it even if they tried. Only me.'

It was a matter of weeks since I returned home when Rebecca came to me in the middle of the night and told me of her wish to end her immortality spell. She had lived long enough and wanted to join her family in whatever counts as the beyond.

I tried to change her mind. I pleaded with her not to end it. But her heart had been broken for far too long. She had lived alone for five centuries and was no longer interested in prolonging her time in this world without the people she loved.

That, and she had learned the horrific truth of what had happened to her daughter at the hands of Grayson and Theo. She could not live with it and told me she believed her daughter Rose was in the afterlife and that all she could think about was seeing her again.

She told me the world had its Arcane now that I was here. That she was no longer needed. That she was tired.

So I helped her end her immortality. Gabriel discovered her back at her cottage the following day. She had taken a poison and fell into her next life peacefully, holding one of the many pictures she had drawn of her family close to her chest.

'Rebecca shared her knowledge with the others whilst I was away,' I tell Connor. 'She helped teach control and understanding of magic and the responsibility that comes with it. She shared a few spells and potions and wrote many of them down in a journal anyone could read. Not just me. But I have seen those books. There is nothing dark in them.'

'And when we got here, we knew nothing of the creatures that inhabited this realm. But in my studies, I have discovered over fifty magical species. That the hair of a sprite mixed with a cat's saliva can cure the hiccups and that ingesting a specific mushroom under the full moon can help you recall memories from infancy.'

'How did you even figure that out?' I ask, struggling to imagine a scenario where that would possibly arise.

'Don't ask. My point is that you learn a lot if you study something enough. And most of what you learn is something you had no intention of discovering.' He drags his fingers through his hair. 'This is Dark Magic. Vampires stole blood, giving them immortal life and a never-ending hunger. In the dark ages, witches would eat the brains of the recently dead to learn the locations of their hidden wealth.'

'Gross...'

'Yeah. If someone stole something from the unicorn, it could point to what they want. Taking blood usually gives some kind of life. Stealing eyes can help people to see hidden truths. A tongue can give the ability to control.'

'It can?'

'I'm talking Dark Magic here, Lilly. This stuff takes years to learn. Decades to prepare your body for. You know yourself; you know how to do magic. The knowledge is in your head. But your body isn't as caught up, which is why your eyes are bloodshot, and you're so pale, you look a little corpse-like.'

'Thanks.'

'Anytime,' he smirks. 'If we discover what they took from the unicorn, it might tell us what they want to achieve. Why the missing are missing. I'm sure you're right. It must be connected. Nothing good happens when you take magic from another creature's life source.'

'What do you think they are trying to do?'

'Your guess is as good as mine. Dark Magic ranges from poison, to necromancy, to soul-stealing, to curses and hexes, to death and-'

'I get the idea. Any guesses as to what kind of Dark Magic would need something from a unicorn?'

'Well, considering that the unicorn is the purest creature in this realm, I can only guess at something highly unnatural. Something we don't want to happen.' He scratches the back of his neck, deep in thought. 'Will you take me to the creature tomorrow? You should rest first, but I'd like to find out what was taken from her as soon as possible. That might give me an indication of what they're planning.'

'Of course.'

There's a slight moan from his tent. We both spin around to look at it.

'You're here with a guy?' I ask in a whisper. 'Who?'

'Erm...' Connor gets to his feet, looking extremely uncomfortable.

'You were aware that someone is in your tent, right?' I ask. 'Because you look surprised.'

'Yeah... yeah, of course, it's just-'

The man in the tent lets out a violent cry and I scream as the flames in the fire pit swell to triple their size and change colour, throwing Connor and me to the ground.

As I fumble my way back to my feet, Connor has already started sprinting towards the tent and is throwing open the door.

'It's okay,' he soothes. 'You're okay. Hey, look at me! You're okay, I promise.'

Just out of sight in the tent's darkness, the man is desperately sobbing with panicked breathing. Their trembling hands grip Connor's shoulders, their fingertips digging into him.

I stand and slowly make my way closer.

'Am I?' he wails. 'Am I still okay? Am I still me?'

'You're still you,' Connor insists. 'I promise. You're right here. Look at me. You're not going anywhere.'

The man throws his arms around Connor and buries his face into his neck, sobbing desperately. As he does, the fire calms and returns to normal.

My footsteps make the leaves rustle, and his head shoots up.

Our eyes meet.

'Lilly?' he whispers, tears streaming down his face. 'W-what are you doing here?' His dark brown hair is cut short and his equally dark brown eyes swim with tears.

'Bias?' I reply, just as taken aback. 'I could ask you the same thing.' I rush towards him and wrap him in a hug. 'I've been worried sick about you.'

Chapter 12

Bias quickly wipes the tears from his cheeks as he steps back.

'What... what are you doing up here?' he asks again, clearing his throat. 'Is everything okay? Is Callie alright? What's happened?'

'I needed to talk to Connor about something. That's all. Everyone is fine, I promise. It was you and Connor we were worried about.'

The panic in his eyes is painful to witness. As is the suffering he still endures every day, haunted by the horrendous deeds of his Broken past.

'W-why are you worried about us?' he asks.

'Because no one knew where to find you. You just took off.' I give him a light smack on his arm. 'Again.'

'It's just... just a bad couple of days.'

Connor stands at his side and rests his hand on Bias's arm.

'I sometimes invite Bias to come on trips with me when he needs some time alone,' Connor tells me. 'It's no big deal.'

'I wish you would have told someone.' I take Bias's hand in mine. His palms are sweaty and he's still trembling. 'Are they still bad?' I ask. 'The nightmares?'

He gives a little nod.

'I had a nightmare today at the lake,' I tell him. 'I woke up to find the river and a dozen rocks floating above all our heads.'

'I'm sorry,' he whispers.

'Don't ever be sorry. You and I are haunted by the same monsters. It's not our fault that what happened in the past happened. I wish you would stop blaming yourself for things that had nothing to do with you.'

I say the words I've heard spoken to me a thousand times.

'I'll stop when you stop,' he replies, his body relaxing. 'Pretty sure I've heard Gabriel tell you that exact same thing.'

'Maybe we should listen to him then.'

His lip trembles. 'I'm so afraid that he'll come back. The thought of *him* here with you all... I would rather die than-'

'He won't come back, Bias. He won't. We won't let him.'

'That's right,' Connor agrees. 'We won't let him, and neither will you.'

I glance at Connor as I notice that they're holding hands.

Connor blushes as I smile softly.

I knew that they were close. I could see the strength of their friendship as soon as I arrived here, and Gabriel told me how wonderful an influence Connor had been for his younger brother.

Connor is such a calming soul. So patient and kind. Full of understanding and trust. It's no wonder Bias gravitated towards him after they all arrived here.

Connor was there for me through so many hideous times. Like an anchor in a storm. He gets that from his wonderful mother, and I'm so glad that Bias finds some peace with him.

I rest my hand on Bias's cheek. His lip trembles more as he leans into my touch.

I hate the guilt he carries. I loathe the misery he feels every single day.

'You're not going anywhere, Tobias. And you know what? Neither am I. Now come and have some of Mama Quinn's pie and tell me all about Connor's conquest for dragons.'

Bias slowly smiles. 'You mean he didn't tell you?'

I look between the two, both looking extremely mischievous.

'Tell me what?'

⚜ ⚜

'I just... I can't believe that you actually found one!' I gasp, peering into the moss-lined box before me, admiring the tiny baby dragon curled up in a ball and sleeping soundly in the corner.

It's barely big enough to fill my hand if I were to hold it. Its skin is a mix of deep blues and purples with a glimmer of silver speckling its tail.

'How did you find it?'

Connor leans in and slowly runs his finger down its spine.

'I was sure I spotted a couple of dragons around here, flying in and out of the cove. But every time I followed them here, I couldn't find any trace. I started to think that they could somehow enchant their nests with something. The only real sighting of a dragon was on the day you returned to us six months ago.'

He shrugs and continues looking at the little creature, utterly besotted.

'I found this little guy at the base of the cliffs. He wasn't moving and was barely breathing yesterday evening. You see here?' Connor gestures to one side of its body.

'Oh... poor thing,' I whisper, looking at the seriously deformed wing. 'Was it in an accident?'

'No. He was born that way. I guess that mum either abandoned him or tossed him from the nest. Animals do that sometimes when a child isn't exactly how they want them to be. They leave them behind to die and move on to their next attempt at furthering their bloodline.'

'Will he be okay?' I ask, reaching in and caressing the little thing myself, unable to resist the urge to touch an actual dragon. Especially a cute mini one like this.

The creature gives a little trill and curls around my finger on contact.

'Oh my goodness. I think my ovaries just vibrated,' I squeak, watching it nuzzle against my hand.

'Tell me about it,' Connor agrees. 'I think he'll be okay. Bias caught some fish earlier. We gave it to him, and he perked up a little, but we don't know how long he was out there on his own. We're keeping a close eye on him, and when he's strong enough, we'll let him go.'

Both Bias and I share a look. I can't see Connor happily releasing this little creature into the wild. Not without some severe tears and prising it from his fingers.

'Lilly,' Bias says. I look up at him and see the worry on his face once more. 'I'm thrilled to see you. But why are you here?' He asks the question with dread. 'There must be a reason for your late-night trek all the way up here. And I can see that you're magically exhausted.'

Connor and I share an uneasiness.

Bias was around before the loss of magic. He's much more familiar with spells and potions than either of us.

Perhaps he will know something.

'Something happened today,' I tell him. 'Maybe you can help.'

Bias listens as I tell him all that happened. The missing people from the village. The death of the unicorn. The mysterious cloaked figure and his knife.

He says the same as Connor. Dark Magic. But he will need to know precisely what was taken from the unicorn to have a guess at knowing the purpose of its murder.

'I should really get going,' I sigh. 'It's late.'

'I don't think that's such a good idea,' Bias tells me.

'Why not?'

'Because it's late. It's dark. And you have already stretched your body's limit with magic doing your leapfrog over here. Your eyes are bloodshot, and I am concerned that you might not reach the destination you would be aiming for due to magical exhaustion and end up entirely elsewhere. Lost and alone. There is also a man with a scythe on the loose, missing witches and a dead unicorn.' He raises his brow.

'I don't want the others to worry.'

'Connor's parents have gone to your house. They would have told them that you are with him. They know you are safe. Get some rest and we can all return together in the morning. What do you say?'

I hesitate.

'I think he's right,' Connor agrees. 'Mum and Dad are at yours. Jensen and Amara too. I imagine Gabriel and Collins are also back from their investigations in the village. Callie is well looked after, and no one will thank you for risking your health and safety trying to get back. Stay with us for the rest of the night.'

Their hopeful eyes shine in the light of the fire, and I know they're right. A few hours of sleep will give me the boost I need to recover.

'Okay,' I agree, making them both relax into smiles. 'I don't suppose you have anything for a headache, do you? Preferably not from cat spit?'

'As a matter of fact, I do,' Connor declares. 'Ginger tea. I'll make you some.'

I sip on the tea he serves, nibble at his mother's pie, and feel the pull of sleep weighing me down.

As my eyes start to close, a blanket is draped over me, and a makeshift pillow made from a folded-up jumper is placed under my head.

'Thank you,' I mutter, too weary to open my eyes.

'My pleasure, Lilly,' Bias whispers in reply.

I fall asleep to their soft voices talking late into the night. And it's a wonderous soundtrack to drift off to.

To them happy. To them content.

To them safe.

Chapter 13

The distant sound of thundering hooves makes me open my eyes. I'm on the floor of the camp, facing the dying embers of the fire.

The sound gets louder.

Bias is the first on his feet, running ahead of me with flames burning on his hands, ready to fight whoever is charging toward us. Connor is quick to stand at his side, fists clenched. Both men stand firm.

I blink a couple of times.

Am I still dreaming?

The long grass starts to move, and out rushes a horse before it skids to a stop.

My eyes widen at the sudden sight of the beast which rears on its hind legs and lets out a furious neigh.

I sit, ready to throw off my blanket and defend us from this intruder.

But the horse lands and I see atop it a man, panting from the effort of a strenuous ride. His eyes land on me in an instant, and he leaps down.

'Gabriel?' I ask, rubbing my eyes. 'What...'

The boys step aside, allowing Gabriel through as he charges toward me. His jaw is rigid in a tight line and his entire body is tensed as he storms closer.

'What part of stay home and rest did you struggle to understand, huh?'

'Don't be mad. I'm sorry I left. It was-' Gabriel falls to his knees before I can fully sit or finish explaining myself. He pulls me into his chest, wrapping his arms around me in a powerful hug.

'Are you determined to give me a fucking heart attack?!' he complains. 'What the hell were you thinking? For fuck's sake, woman. I just got you back. You can't be running off on your own looking for lunatics with knives who are going around slaughtering fucking unicorns!' He lets out a long sigh and breathes me in as he holds me. 'My heart is about ready to burst through my chest here, Beautiful. I'm ready to drop with goddamn worry.'

'I'm sorry,' I tell him, reaching up and knotting my fingers in his dark hair. 'I planned to come back, but I was just so tired. How did you get here so fast?'

He sits back on his feet and sweeps my hair clear from my face, looking me over with both relief and concern.

'I got back shortly after Connor's parents arrived at the cottage. They told me you went to see them and carried on down the coast to look for Connor. I didn't even bother dismounting the horse. I just went at full speed to where they told me you would be.'

The horse gives a tired grunt and lays down, ready to have a well-earned sleep.

Gabriel pulls me in once more and melds himself around me.

'I'm okay,' I assure him. 'Everything is fine.'

'Everything is not fine.' Gabriel looks up at the others. His eyes land on Bias. 'Thank fuck you're okay. We've been looking for you.'

'We're fine,' Bias nods. 'I'm still me, so there's no need to worry.'

Gabriel gets to his feet and pulls Bias into a hug.

'I'm not worried about that, you prat. I have no concerns about your Break in the slightest. I was worried you were hurt or alone and sinking in bad thoughts. I thought... I was scared that you were hurt. That they might have taken you too.' Gabriel tuts and holds him tighter. Bias hugs him right back. 'Don't disappear like that again, Bias.' He releases him and gives him a firm whack on his shoulder before pointing angrily at all three of us. 'If you lot can't behave, I will have no other choice but to put a tracking spell on you all. I seriously have no idea how much more my heart can take. We stick together. All of us. You got that?'

He looks at me, and I nod. He looks at Connor who also nods.

Bias hesitates.

'I mean it, brother,' Gabriel states. 'You're not on your own here, okay? If you're in pain, we want to help.'

'The pain I feel is my own fault. I don't want to bring down your time together. You and Lilly have only just reunited. I'm in the way.'

'We're a family. All of us. So quit saying stupid shit like that. If you wanna take off, come over and talk to us first.' He pats Bias affectionately on the cheek. 'I've only just got you back too, don't forget. Our house is big enough for your crazy arse to come over any time. All the time. Don't think otherwise. Ever.'

With a humble smile, Bias nods.

'What happened at the village?' I ask Gabriel. 'Did you find anything?'

Gabriel turns to me. I really dislike the look on his face.

'What? I dare ask. 'Did you find them? Are they okay?

'We erm...' He clears his throat and stands a little taller. 'We didn't. No. But we did go to the location of the slaughtered animals the girl Megan mentioned. And erm...'

'What?'

'There were a lot of dead animals. All with missing body parts or organs. We think it's someone messing about with-'

'Dark Magic,' I finish.

'Yeah. Yeah, someone is messing with Dark Magic.'

'That's bad. That's... that's very bad.' I look at them all. 'And what about our people? Are they still missing? What if they're being carved up and having bits stolen for this Dark Magic?'

'The Council are all over it. We'll find them.'

'We should go back to the village. To the site of the slaughtered animals. To-'

Gabriel clamps his hands down on my shoulders, stopping me from charging off.

'There's nothing to be done for now. Not for us. And not for you.'

'I'm responsible for-'

'No. We are all responsible. All of us. And if you don't slow the fuck down and calm your pace, you will end up seriously hurting yourself. All you need to do now is take a breath and trust me.'

'We need to go back.'

'You're not ready to whoosh yet. Your eyes are still bloodshot.'

'Then we ride.'

Gabriel looks at the horse currently snoring across the camp.

'I don't think that's going to happen either. Not yet, anyway.' He rests his hands on my hips. 'We will find them. I promise. But right now, you need to stop. You need to recharge. You need to come with me.'

'Why? Where are we going?'

'I want to show you something.' He smiles. 'Come on.'

He takes my hand and leads me away from the camp. As he looks back, he shows me that wicked half-smile and as I stumble, still cumbersome from sleep, he spins on his heel and tosses me over his shoulder.

'What the hell are you doing?' I laugh as he carries me into the grass.

'You'll see,' he says, slapping my backside as he strides onwards, letting out a soft chuckle. 'You'll see.'

Chapter 14

The sound of the ocean gets louder as Gabriel carries me, still over his shoulder, down a slope.

The grass turns to sand, and soon we're on the beach. He stops and lowers me, gently sliding me down his front until my feet are back on the ground.

I peer up at him. He surveys me, his vivid blue eyes watching me.

'There you are,' he says softly. 'In my arms. As you should be.'

He rests the tips of his fingers beneath my chin and tilts my head up. His soft lips land on mine and claim a kiss. A tender, soft, loving kiss.

His tongue glides across mine, making my skin erupt in goose bumps.

'Let's take a swim,' he whispers, nodding to the ocean. He takes the hem of my shirt and pulls it over my head.

I pull off his shirt too and unfasten his trousers. He watches me closely and enjoys my smirk when I see him in all his glory.

As he lowers my trousers, he falls to his knees, guiding out each one of my feet with purpose.

He stays on his knees and trails his hands up my legs, stopping when they reach my ass.

Gabriel looks up at me, the corner of his mouth hitching into a smile, and without looking away, he leans in and runs his tongue between my legs.

'Fuck...' I hiss as he seals his lips around me, gently flicking his tongue and softly sucking.

My fingers grab at his hair, and I throw back my head, moaning as he works his sweet magic.

His fingers glide around my backside and he pins me to him before his fingers find their way between my thighs, teasing my entrance.

'*Fuck-fuck-fuck*...' I moan, biting my lip.

He eases his fingers inside me, one from each hand, and slowly works them in and out. In and out. With his knees, he nudges my legs a little further apart and buries his face deeper between my legs, moaning as he does.

But it's not enough. I push him down into the sand on his back.

He looks up at me as I stand over him, naked and wet, hungry for him and his touch.

'That's the most beautiful thing I have ever seen,' he admires as I place a foot by either side of his head. 'And it's all fucking mine. Take a seat, beautiful. I'm fucking starving.'

I turn and get on all fours, my legs wide and a knee either side of his head. I lean down and take him into my mouth as he buries his face between my legs.

I relish in every single fucking second. Feeling his tongue and lips. The pressure of his fingers easing in and out of me as I use my mouth on him to make him moan.

The waves start to reach us and sweep past our hot bodies. He moves his hips in time with my mouth, slowly fucking me as I welcome the blissful feeling of satisfaction ebbing closer and closer.

As my release approaches and my moans get wilder, he speeds up, both with his tongue and his thrusts into my mouth.

I draw back and cry out, my release exploding from my body wave after wave. As soon as it slows, Gabriel is up and gets me on all fours, facing us both out to the ocean. He wastes no time and drives himself into me from behind, hissing with pleasure when he's fully buried deep inside me.

With his arms wrapped around my belly, he lifts me. I reach back and grip his neck as his hands cup my breasts.

'You're so fucking beautiful,' he gasps with each firm thrust. 'You're so fucking perfect. You're so fucking mine.'

His hands caress, pinch and grab before he sinks one of his fingers into my mouth. I suck them hard, making him let out a dark laugh behind me.

'Good girl,' he soothes, removing them from my mouth and resting them on my clit.

'Gabriel...' I whisper.

'Yes, wife?' he asks, picking up the pace a little.

'I absofuckinglutely love you.'

'I absofuckinglutely love you more.'

I look back at him. His eyes bore into mine, lust-filled and devious.

We never look away, so entrapped by each other's gaze it's impossible to even think about looking at anything else.

'I'm close,' I whisper.

He speeds up a little more and steals another kiss. Our eyes are still open, and he catches my desperate moans with his tongue.

The sky starts to flicker as red lightning stirs from behind the clouds.

I moan louder.

Water starts to rise from the sea in tiny droplets.

I dig my fingernails into his neck as the pressure inside becomes unbearable.

He pinches my nipple and grips my breast and I come completely undone, crying out in pleasure as I find my release in his arms.

His eyes darken, and that delicious smile of his grows.

'Keep coming,' he orders, compelling my body to obey.

Wave after wave of pleasure continues to expel itself from me. I throw back my head and rest it on his shoulder.

He leans into my ear.

'Keep coming,' he instructs.

I do... it just goes on and on. My eyes fill with tears, and I could cry at the sheer euphoria.

'Keep..' he pants in my ear. 'Coming...'

'Oh my God!!!' I cry, dizzy from the never-ending orgasm.

'Yes, my Goddess?' he replies.

I feel the hold of his power leave and I ride out the final wave of orgasmic bliss before he pulls himself free and turns me to face him. He sits and guides me back onto him.

'I will never tire of how fucking good you feel,' he says, letting out a wanton breath as I ease myself onto him.

I seal my lips around his as I ride him hard, rocking my hips in time with his as the sea water rushes past our bodies.

His hands clamp down hard on my waist as he pulls me onto him harder... harder... HARDER!

And when he draws close, I hold his face in my hands.

'Wait for me,' I pant, my forehead on his as I feel the build of my release rushing closer. '*Fuuuuuccccck*!'

He groans loudly as I come around him, almost clawing at his skin as I relish in every delicious second.

He slows, as do I, and I slump into his shoulder as he catches his breath.

My eyes turn black, and I mimic his dirty smirk.

I lean in and whisper... 'Again. Right now.'

'My fucking pleasure, wife.'

Chapter 15

G abriel holds me as he wades into the ocean. My legs are wrapped around his waist and my head rests on his shoulder as he takes us deeper and deeper into the sea.

The cool water is refreshing on our hot skin, and the sun slowly rising in the horizon is a wonder to behold.

'I'm so proud of you,' he says. 'What you did, with The Stolen and coming to find the guys, you're a natural leader. A protector. A defender.'

'I thought you were mad at me.'

'Mad you left without me. Not mad you left.' He kisses my cheek. 'But to the fool who attacked you, well, they're going to wish they had never been born.'

'Do you think that they're trying to re-open the Veil?' I ask him, my eyes on the glowing horizon. 'Do you think that's what this is all about?'

'Maybe.'

'We have to do something about this, Gabriel. If they succeed, they could bring the whole human world down on us.' I tense around him. 'I can't go back to that life. None of us can. Callie can't.'

'The Bloodstones are dead, Lilly. The only real power they had was put there by Rebecca Hooper and then harnessed by you. The Hooper witches are the real power here. Not the Bloodstones. Whatever comes, we'll face it together,' he promises. 'All of us. The entire Council are looking for the missing witches, and if there is a threat, we will deal with it as one.'

His hands grip me a little harder as I nod.

'Come on. Let's get back to camp and get a couple of hours sleep before heading home.'

He turns and wades out of the water, carrying me in his arms to the beach and back to our discarded clothes.

We climb the steep pathway up to Connor's camp, Gabriel holding my hand and leading the way. He turns back to me.

'So Connor and Bias...'

'Connor and Bias.' I reply.

'Is that more than a friendship, do you think?'

'I think that Bias finds comfort in Connor. I think he finds peace. Connor's an extremely kind and sweet man. Very patient and always looks at the positives. I found that a tremendous comfort on some of my darker times at The Orchard.'

'But Connor's a guy.'

'No shit,' I laugh. 'I don't think a silly thing like gender ever really bothered Bias. He wasn't shy about experiment-ing when we were-' I shut the hell up. Why would I even bring that up? I wait for his reaction. For Gabriel to turn with a scowl or a glare.

But he doesn't. He just carries on.

'Funny thing is, when we were kids, I always thought that Bias preferred guys to girls. I was convinced, but with our family it was better to keep that to yourself. If Bias ever had feelings for a man, he never would have said.

Finding acceptance in my house was like finding a virgin in a brothel. Except for our mother, of course. She would have screamed her pride from the rooftops.' He looks at me with a sad little smile as he thinks of his mother. 'She would have fucking loved you.'

'You think?'

'I know. I'm glad they've found each other. I'm glad Bias has-'

'Gabriel!' I stop suddenly, yanking at his hand.

'What?' What's the matter?'

'I... I can't see...' I tighten my grip on his hand, swallowed suddenly in pitch blackness. 'I can't see! Gabriel... Something's-'

I scream and grab my head, howling in pain as I get bombarded with images. They slam into my brain with relentless violence, forcing their way into the deepest recesses of my mind.

I haven't had a vision since returning. I wasn't sure that the realm had manifested yet, but it sure as shit has now.

The agony expels a blast of Telekinetic energy from my body. The edge of the cliff trembles and the ground beneath our feet crumbles into dust.

I fall.

⚡⚡⚡⚡⚡ ⚡⚡⚡⚡⚡

I stand in the doorway, watching a woman on all fours screaming with all her might. Her sobs echo all around the darkness of this old bedroom.

There's a single bed with an old sheet crumpled on it and blood on the mattress. The woman crawls slowly towards it and reaches up. Her hands fist the sheet, and she lets out another wail of pure pain.

I take a step closer, afraid of what I may see when I get nearer.

She grunts and pants as she gets herself on her knees and grips the bed.

She takes a few deep breaths and then screams.

When I reach the bed, I stop. My mouth falls open as I see her.

Sweat is pouring down her face. Tears are streaming down her cheeks.

'Mum?' I whisper, looking at the young woman before me.

A woman who I know only from my memories and night-mares.

The woman who tortured me as a small child with pain in the hopes that she would spark my magic into life.

The woman who tried to drown me in the bathtub.

She looks down and rests her hands between her legs, and with a final scream, she gasps in relief.

From under her nightdress, I hear the first cry of a new born baby.

She trembles as she peers down. Even now, there's no love on that woman's face.

She fucking sneers at me as she sees my face for the first time, peeking out from under her nightdress.

Her child made for no other reason than to have magic.

She puts me, still wailing and trembling, on the floor, hidden under her night dress.

She closes her eyes and just stays there, slowly breathing.

I can't cope with the sound of me crying, brand new, cold and scared!

Not at all.

I think of Callie, and I just can't understand how a mother can bear to hear such suffering.

I reach down to lift the baby from the floor. Foolish, as I can touch nothing here. I'm just looking, forced into this moment through magic.

'Pick her up!' I yell.

My mother ignores me.

Both of me.

'PICK HER UP!!'

As I go to strike her, the image shifts.

The world around me fades into smoke and reforms into another.

Darkness. There's not a single beam of natural light to be seen.

Hundreds of candles flicker all around me, casting an eerie orange glow.

I'm in the middle of a cavern. The roof reaches high and is lost to sight. Jagged rocks protrude from every surface and in the very centre...

'The final Bloodstone,' I gasp.

It's clear and broken from when I completed it all those years ago.

There's a hideous screech in my head, like nails on a chalkboard and metal scraping against metal. The vision shifts and distorts, switching between the empty space to something else.

Something dark.

Now, bodies lie on the floor, spread out evenly in a very particular pattern, surrounding the Bloodstone column.

Another shift, and their bodies are carved up. Their chests are open. Their bellies are gaping holes. Blood pools around them.

In the centre is a hooded figure. In his hand is a scythe dripping with blood.

He stands at a long table, atop which is a mixture of bloody organs.

He's chanting, speaking ancient words.

There's a groan. I look down, and to my horror, I see that the man lying at my feet, gutted and bleeding, is still alive.

They all are.

As the man chants, the blood seeping from the seven victims on the floor begins to move, flowing with purpose.

It forms a seven-pointed star. At the very centre is the Bloodstone.

As the blood reaches it, the Bloodstone slowly starts to change. From the ground up, it becomes that familiar deep red swirling with black. But this time, it's like thick tar, oozing on the outside and dripping to the floor.

It hisses like acid and scorches the ground.

I lift my gaze, horrified at the vision I'm being shown.

And as I do, I come face to face with the darkened shadow beneath the hood of the killer.

He pulls back his hand, and with a forceful thrust, he buries the scythe deep in my belly.

I feel it. I feel every inch of its steel tearing its way through my body.

I feel his hot breath land on my skin and the warmth of my blood as it spills down my legs. He withdraws the blade and sinks his hand inside me before plucking out something and clasping it in his blood-drenched fist.

I grab his wrist. My hand looks burnt. My fingers are blackened and scarred.

I watch him return to the table.

And I fall to the floor, and I die.

Chapter 16

My eyes spring open. I'm still screaming. Screaming in pain and in sheer terror. Gabriel is yelling at me, begging me to wake up. To stop thrashing!

And I soon realise why.

I've blasted half the damn cliff away, and we're currently dangling at least fifty metres off the beach. Gabriel has hold of a very precarious rock and is gripping my wrist hard as he tries to keep me from plummeting down.

'I can't hold on,' he yells, straining as his fingers slip. There's nothing for us to grab onto, just a sheer drop. 'Lilly—'

I reach up and secure my hand around his wrist, and just as he lets go of the rock, I channel my magic.

We both crash-land back at Connor's camp. Every bone in my body screams from the harsh impact and the air is knocked clear from my lungs. Worse than that is the crippling pain in my head, bad enough to make it hard to even open my eyes.

'Jesus Christ!' Connor exclaims, still sitting on the log by the fire, a mug of coffee in his hands and his eyes wide in shock. 'What the fuck happened to you two?'

My brain pounds so much that all I can do is roll on my side and clasp at my head.

'She's had a vision,' Gabriel says, struggling to his knees and crawling closer to me.

They all rush to my side.

Gabriel rests his hands on my back.

'Watch her head,' he says. 'Give her a minute.'

But we don't have a minute. I slam my hand on his head and share my vision, showing him everything.

Gabriel falls back, panting and horrified.

'W-what the fuck was that?' he stammers.

'My birth,' I tell him, groaning at the discomfort speaking causes. 'The woman at the beginning, she was my mum. That was her giving birth to me. And the end...' I struggle to say anything else as the world spins wildly around me.

'What?' Bias asks. 'What was in the end?'

'The man... the man with the scythe.' Gabriel swallows. He eases me up and cradles me in his arms. 'In the vision... he...'

'What?' asks Bias, looking harrowed by the terror on his brother's face. 'What does he do?'

Gabriel's arms tighten around me, and he says in a whisper...

'He m-murders Lilly.'

Chapter 17

After some vomiting and violent retching, I finally manage to return to my feet, which is made harder by the three of them determined to smother me.

'I can stand on my own. I don't need you pawing at me,' I snap.

'Well, excuse me for being freaked the fuck out, Beautiful!' Gabriel bites back, grabbing my arm despite my efforts to dodge him. 'I just saw the love of my life gutted like a fucking fish, so pardon me for being a little overprotective.'

'Visions aren't as cut and dry as that. You know that. Connor, do you have some water?' I ask.

Nodding, Connor quickly runs to the tent and returns with a flask. I down the lot and rest my hand on my forehead, wishing the thumping from inside would end.

'I think it was pretty clear what you saw,' Gabriel scoffs.

'We need to go to the Bloodstone,' I insist.

'NO!'
'NO!'
'NO!'

All three bellow the word at me.

'If some lunatic has captured our people and is about to slaughter them, do you not think perhaps we should try to stop him? If he's messing with the Veil, we can't just stand by and let him.'

'Yes. Let's take you to the place you just DIED!' Gabriel roars in frustration. 'Shall we take a knife for him too? So he doesn't bloody up his own? Maybe we can put a goddamn ribbon on your ass since we're handing it over so freely.'

'I didn't risk everything and lose five years of my life so some lunatic can tear down the Veil and throw the world and our people into chaos.'

'Let's calm down,' Bias interrupts before Gabriel can argue. 'Lilly's Sight magic has only just returned. Visions are tricky. They can mean a million things.' He holds out his hand to me. 'May I see it?'

I hold out my hand and show Bias the vision. When I open my eyes again, he's gone ashen.

'Well, that bit at the end was pretty clear, wasn't it...' Bias murmurs, stepping back and throwing sidelong glances at Gabriel. 'That was erm... it was...'

'It was my wife being killed. Yeah.'

Connor rests his hand on Bias's back.

'It was extremely disjointed, flicking between the past and the present like that. Why show you your birth and your death?'

'Well, as you have the most experience with the realm of Sight, I hoped you could tell us!'

'Gabriel!' I snap. 'This isn't his fault. Don't be a dick.'

Gabriel drags his hands through his hair and seals his lips with a growl.

'Why would we need to see her birth and death?' Connor asks Bias, much calmer than Gabriel seems capable of right now.

'I... I don't know. Sight is about showing a glimpse of what needs to be seen. And seeing as Lilly's magic is so new, and this was her first vision since getting her magic back, her ability to handle and understand them are in their infancy. It will take time for them to become clear.'

'Real helpful,' Gabriel mutters.

'We need to check that the Bloodstones are secure.' I stand and face them, smoothing down my hair and trying to look like I have myself together.

'They are secure.' Gabriel helps me as I wobble a little. 'I told you before. They're being guarded by a member of the council at all times. And you are not to go near the Bloodstones until this lunatic is dealt with. Do you hear me?' His desperate eyes look into mine as he holds my chin in between his thumb and forefinger. 'Please, Beautiful. Please don't put yourself in danger.'

Reluctantly, I nod. 'Why would he need the seven witches?' I ask. 'Why kill the unicorn?'

'We should go to the unicorn and see what was taken from her,' Bias says. 'In the vision, there was a table. An altar of sorts. If we find out what ingredients he's using for this Dark Magic, we may get a head start on finding a way to stop his plans.'

I get to my feet and brush off the dirt and leaves.

'We go now. Yes?' I ask.

They all nod. Gabriel included.

'Get your stuff together,' I tell them. 'We leave in five.'

Chapter 18

Connor wails like a heartbroken beast when he sees the unicorn's body. He runs to its side, dropping to his knees.

'Who... who could do such a thing? *Why*? Oh, you wonderful, beautiful thing.'

Its eyes stare at me lifelessly. Its fur is stained red with old blood. The life that once flourished around it has decayed so much, it's all but crumbled.

I look around uneasily, very aware that the last time I was here, so was the killer.

'Can you see what was taken?' Gabriel asks, his eyes scouring every inch of the forest as he grips my hand in his.

'I... I'll need to look inside,' Connor replies, shaking his head and lost to grief for the poor creature.

He looks up at Bias standing beside him. A pleading look swims in his eyes. To carve up this creature, even dead, is more than he can bear.

Bias kneels at his side.

'I'll help you. Just tell me where to cut.'

Bias pulls out a knife and gives Connor a reassuring nod. From inside Connor's collar, a small, scaled head with little black eyes peer out.

It's the baby dragon. He whimpers as he sees the unicorn. And when Bias presses the blade into the wound site, reopening the cut I sealed, he retreats into the safety of the collar.

I admit I struggle to watch.

Gabriel takes my hands and turns me away so that all I can see are his eyes.

The squelching and Connor's pained groans are nauseating, and I wince as I hear them.

Gabriel never flinches. He refuses to break our gaze.

Moments pass. Connor continues to grimace and grunt as he seeks out his answer.

He goes quiet.

'What in the...' he finally whispers.

Gabriel peers over my shoulder. I follow his lead and turn to Connor. His hands drip with congealed blood as he slowly turns to face us.

I have never seen him so pale.

'What is it?' I ask.

'She was erm...' Connor clears his throat. 'She was pregnant.'

'W-what?'

He looks back at her. A tear slides down his cheek. 'This unicorn was pregnant. A couple of months or so. He... the killer took her unborn baby.'

'What does that mean? What does that point to?'

'Bloodlines. To take something like this... it's bloodlines. Genealogy. Tapping into traits handed down from mother to child, tapping into DNA and manipulating it.'

'Why? Why would anyone do that?' I ask.

Gabriel shuffles as he looks at Bias. The two share a look.

'Josiah...' Gabriel whispers as Bias nods.

'Who?' I butt in.

'Centuries ago,' Gabriel starts. 'Back before magic was stolen and the Veil was put up, Josiah Theydon was a Coven Leader. He practised Dark Magic and started teaching it to his people. He basically invented it.'

'Why?'

'Same reason as always. Power. To take what he had and make it more than anyone else's. To have more wealth. Control. To be feared.'

'Josiah found a way to awaken other magics in his bloodline,' Bias continues. 'He tapped into every realm of power that his ancestors had passed onto him. Those dormant realms from long ago. If his great great great grandfather had Elemental magic, he could tap into that.'

Gabriel looks at me. 'He managed to awaken four realms of magic. All through Blood and Dark Magic. He took the life force and body parts from others and wielded his own brand of twisted magic over them. By taking the unborn life of a magical creature and consuming the life force of those who had access to the magic he desired.'

'He could do that?' I gasp.

'Our grandfather, along with several other coven leaders, gathered together and killed Josiah,' Bias says. 'They knew this unnatural magic had to be extinguished. It messed with the order of nature.'

'How do you mean?'

They look at the rotten vegetation around us.

'It was like a poison spreading across the land. Turning everything it touched to ash. To decay. To sickness. Creatures of peace turned vicious or were born deformed and twisted. Our grandfather and the others had no choice. Josiah's Coven needed to be stopped before their darkness spread.'

'Stopped?' I dare ask.

'They wiped out his entire Coven,' Gabriel says simply. 'But clearly, someone here knows Josiah's secrets.'

'So, maybe this isn't about opening the Veil,' I ponder aloud. 'Maybe this is just about gaining more power. Either way, they have to be stopped. This world is ours. I will never let them take it and turn it rotten. Never.'

When the brush starts to rustle, everyone turns, ready to fight. Ready to kill.

But it's a friend who explodes into the clearing.

'Clara?' I gasp, watching her stagger towards me with blood seeping down her face. 'What's happened?'

'Y-your cottage!' she pants, pointing into the distance to where my home lies. 'It's under attack. Men with cloaks and knives... they broke in!'

Gabriel and I look at each other, each with sheer terror on our faces.

'Callie...' I whisper.

As we share in our moment of horror, from behind, there's a thump. We both turn to see Bias and Connor on the floor, smothered in the same black smoke I saw last time when the hooded man attacked.

The next thing I see is the same black smoke exploding at Gabriel's and my feet, smothering us completely.

One breath, that's all it takes for me to fall unconscious and hit the ground hard.

Chapter 19

The distorted and distant sound of voices stirs me from unconsciousness. A sharp pain throbs in my skull and the blood pounding through my ears is deafening. As I try to move I realise that I can't. My hands are tied behind my back by rope that pinches tightly into my wrists.

Then I hear a cry. A scared little whimper that has my head up and every one of my senses on high alert. I blink the world into focus.

And my eyes land on Callie straight away.

She's sat in front of me on her knees, dressed in her little nightdress, filthy with dirt. Her hands are tied behind her back and there's a gag in her mouth. Tears stream down her frightened face as she trembles all over.

I fill with ravenous wrath when I notice the bruise on her cheek.

Her eyes are on me. She's calling for me, her words stolen by that rag between her lips. Desperately, she pulls at the rope keeping her tethered to a pillar of stone.

Not just any stone.

To what remains of the final Bloodstone. I look up and all around.

'Shit...' I hiss, pulling against the ropes once more.

We're in the same place the vision showed me. The same place I saw myself die.

To make matters worse, we're not alone.

Surrounding us all, encircling us, are ten others. They're all in long robes with hoods covering their faces. Their hands are together as if in prayer and they hold deep red candles.

I try to go to Callie, but I'm trapped too, tied to a pole with my hands bound behind my back. I try to call my magic, but it doesn't come.

'I wouldn't bother trying to get free.'

The sound of footsteps in the dirt moves closer. I look up as Clara plants herself before me with a disgustingly smug grin.

'Those ropes are tied tight, and thanks to your incredibly generous assistance, you solved our problem of how to contain your magic. I thank you for making your own binding spell. I would not have known how to make one myself. Sadly, trapping magic was never a part of my education. Quite the opposite, in fact.'

She peers over my shoulder with a self-assured smirk. I look and see the small binding spell I made at the side of the river wrapped firmly around my wrist.

When I try to speak, my words are muffled.

Clara kneels and slides the gag down, freeing my mouth.

'What the fuck are you doing?!' I demand, rage shaking my words and panic surging through my veins. 'Where are the others? What have you done to them? Let us go. Right now, or-'

'Or what?' she scoffs. 'I'm sorry. But you are not going to do a thing.' She taps the end of my nose. 'Not a damn thing.'

Thrashing, I try to bite her fucking finger clean off. She merely laughs and gets to her feet, kicking a load of dirt and dust at me as she does.

Clara strolls away towards an altar type of table beside the Bloodstone and Callie.

I look at Callie and do my best to smile. The sheer terror on her face... it breaks my heart into pieces as she glances at all those who stand around us.

'Look at me, baby girl. You look at me. Listen. You are going to be fine, okay? You'll be absolutely fine. I promise.'

'Don't be making promises you can't keep, Arcane.' The low voice that echoes around the chamber is familiar. From behind comes another.

He stops and flashes me a wink.

'Ash,' I snarl, watching him stride towards his mother.

At his hip, tucked into his belt, is the scythe.

'I swear,' I warn. 'If either of you hurt a single hair on my daughter's head, I will skin you both alive. You will wish you were never fucking born!'

Ash chuckles darkly as he carries on towards Clara.

On the altar is a large chalice and a bloodied bowl beside it.

Clara starts grinding up whatever is in the bowl. The crunching mixes with a wet squelching as she works.

'Why are you doing this?' I ask, pulling once more at my bindings. 'What do you want?'

'What do I want?' Ash asks, almost shocked that I would ask such a foolish question. He turns to face me and shakes his head with a disbelieving grimace. 'I want what I'm due.' He points to himself. His grimace turning into an angry sneer. 'What I'm entitled to. What is rightfully mine!'

'More power? Is that all you want, huh? Being in the Council not enough for you? Pathetic.'

'You don't recognise me?' he asks. 'I don't look familiar?'

'You look like a psycho. A soon-to-be-dead psycho,' I spit back.

'So I do look familiar then,' he laughs. 'I take it your precious mother never mentioned me then?'

'My mother?'

'Yes. The dead psycho. Did she ever mention me?'

'No. But then, as you said. Dead. And a psycho. Who the fuck are you?'

'I'm you,' he shrugs. 'Or... I should have been. Everything you have should have been mine by right. Your magic. Your power. Your position-'

'I have no fucking idea who you are, and I don't care. Let us go, and I promise I won't kill you.'

'No one is going anywhere until I get what I want.' He looks around him proudly. 'And you are all going to give it to me. Every single one of you.'

I follow his gaze.

Fuck!

Six others are sprawled out in perfect symmetry, lying still and silent. The five missing witches.

And Gabriel.

'What have you done to them?' I ask. Their eyes flicker open occasionally, but they don't move a muscle.

'A simple enough remedy,' he shrugs. 'Paralyzes them. Makes them compliant.'

'You're the one that brought their disappearance to our attention. Why bother if you're the one who took them?' I stare at Gabriel, wishing his eyes would open.

'The rest of the Council discovered it and brought it to me,' Ash groans. 'If I'd have hidden it, I would have looked suspicious. So I had to play along.' He faces me once more and continues to sneer. 'It should have been mine. You don't deserve all you have.' His eyes narrow. 'That's about to change.'

'And about time too,' comes another voice.

Her voice is soft. And it's one I know well. One I thought had died back in the human world. There are slow and purposeful footsteps, and I watch as she walks around me, placing herself at Ash's side. Her snide smile is just as I remember it. And I hate it just as much now as I ever did.

'Lilly Hooper takes what she wants and cares not one bit who she hurts in the process. She destroys the lives of others and tears them into tiny pieces. It's about time she got a taste of her own medicine.'

'Ava Sinclair,' I snarl, loathing every single fucking breath she takes.

'The one and only,' she grins, flicking her greasy blonde hair over her shoulder and clinging to Ash's arm. She's so thin, I can see her bones protruding through her skin, and her eyes are sunken and dry. She's a far cry from the preened princess I knew. 'Did you miss me?'

'I thought you were dead.'

'You killed me once. I learnt my lesson. Once I got my memories back, I made damn sure I was nowhere near you when you came to finish that spell.'

As she recalls her past, I see a flicker of fear in her eyes.

'How are those memories treating you?' I ask. 'I wonder, which one is your favourite? When I made you drink Hendrix's piss? When I gutted you like a fish and left your insides on your outside? Or when I made you watch as you heard the truth about Toby Smith and how little you meant to him?'

Her eye twitches.

'I admit I am happy it turned out this way,' Ava snarls through clenched teeth. 'I was there when your first child died. Now I get to watch you suffer that torture all over again when brat number two gets what's coming to her.'

Ava glances back at Callie before settling her gaze on me.

I don't know what's worse. The fear, or the rage that stirs at something dark, deep inside me.

Ava smiles up at Ash, just as she used to with Toby.

I shake my head. 'Trust you to latch onto another lunatic.'

Clara gently laughs, still grinding up whatever is in that bowl. 'We are not lunatics, Lilly.' She lifts her head proudly. 'We are visionaries. You and the rest of your so-called Coven. You're primitive. You lack vision. Courage. Creativity.'

'Is that so?' I scoff back.

'Extremely so. Yes. But then, your people always were so scared to push themselves. Terrified to accept your full potential. So closed-minded to the possibilities around you all.'

I look at the bowl with blood dripping down the sides.

'You work with Blood magic. Dark Magic. Your ways were destroyed. Your Coven was decimated.'

'Yes. Before the Veil cut us all off, my Coven worshipped the Blood magics. Embraced it. Used it to make us strong. Make us mighty. We connected with the Arcane Realm in a way you could never comprehend, and your people punished my people for it. As you said, they decimated us.

And because they decimated us, they allowed the humans to defeat witches. We would never have lost the war with the humans if we were there to fight. But you did to us what the humans did to you. And it's payback time, Lilly. We are rebuilding our numbers.' She gestures to the hooded figures stood around us. 'Those you stole from the human world have joined our ranks against you. Well, some of them at least,' she adds. 'But with our promises, more will join our ranks.'

'The Stolen?' I stare hatefully at the hooded figures. 'You scream and shout about how much you hate magic, and you join a Dark Magic coven? Why?'

'They wish to return home. You refuse to send them, so we will. In exchange for their services, of course.'

'The Veil is sealed. I cannot open it.' I look at those surrounding us. 'It's impossible. Whatever lies they have told you, whatever promises they have made about sending you back, I am telling you that it can't be done.'

'It can. And it will. It's time for us to take back our rightful place as the superior witch.' Clara looks at her son with pride. 'With an Arcane Witch, powerful enough to tear down the walls your ancestors built, to lead us.'

'Him?' I scoff. 'You think your son can be an Arcane? Are you delusional? Do you know what an Arcane even is? How they're made?'

'Better than you could ever grasp,' Clara hisses hatefully. 'After all, how do you think it came to be that Hooper's have access to all seven realms of power?'

'You were made, Lilly,' Ava sings cruelly. 'The very first Arcane Witch was made with Dark Magic. With Blood and sacrifice. Your ancestors were part of Clara's ancestors' coven, and when their creation was discovered by great, great, great grandaddy Kendryk, he slaughtered the entire Coven and stole her for himself. For his coven. To further his power and strength.' Ava giggles like a little psycho, bouncing on the balls of her feet. 'You're the offspring of Josiah Theydon. He unlocked his bloodline magic as well as his daughter's. She was the first Hooper Witch.'

'Am I supposed to care?' I reply. 'I don't give a shit where I came from. I'm here now and I'm not going anywhere. This is your last chance. Let us go. You will never get what you want. It's impossible. You can't access all seven realms of power. You will never be an Arcane.'

'An Arcane Witch carries within them the seven realms of power,' Clara replies. 'But to be able to access that power, they must have a child with another witch whom they love and love back.' She turns to Ash, who hasn't stopped glaring murderously at me this whole time. 'But what happens when a Hooper child is born to a loveless union? When a lunatic, desperate for a child with magic, whores her way around the Nomad camp and pushes out a child born without even a hint of love?'

I look at Ash.

'There's no way...' I whisper. 'No... no way!'

'I was six when our mother gave up trying to make my magic come through.' Ash lifts his shirt, showing deep scars on his belly. He turns and reveals countless more on his back. 'He faces me again. 'She gave birth to me in a shack, in the middle of the woods. Pushed me out and kept me alive. That was it. No love. No kindness. Nothing except pain and torment from my first memory to my last as she tried to get my magic to come through. She left me when it became clear I was not what she wanted. Locked me in that shack. Boarded up the windows. And left to try again. She left to have you.' His face contorts in hate. 'I WAS SIX AND SHE LEFT ME THERE TO STARVE!!'

'I didn't know that. And if you think she was any kinder to me, then you're painfully wrong. She tried to kill me. She hurt me too. She was insane!'

'I found him,' Clara says, ignoring my words. 'As I was scavenging in the woods for berries, I came across the cabin and heard him scratching at the door. My Coven, if you could call us that, lived a few miles away. We took him in. The Hooper child abandoned by his mother. Such possibility lay within him. Such potential. To those who know how to harness such gifts, he was a miracle.' She dips her finger into the concoction and puts it in her mouth, sucking it clean. 'To take the life source from another and harness it, gives a power you white witches could never comprehend. My coven barely survived your butchery, but we did survive. Our ancestors passed on their knowledge even after the Veil was put up. They taught all there was to know about our ways. We kept the practice alive, knowing one day, we would have that power once more. Knowledge I shared with my adopted son. A Hooper witch by blood.'

'Your way is evil. You slaughter for your own gain and turn your souls and the world around you black in the process.'

'Coming from you, that's hysterical,' Ava retorts. 'The Broken Arcane.'

'Ava told us you were quite the serial killer back in the day.' Ash adds.

Ava turns to Callie. 'Did you know that, sweetheart? About your precious mummy-'

'You don't get to talk to her!' I spit, burning hot with hatred. 'You don't even get to look at her!'

Callie's eyes refuse to leave me. Even as the others speak and walk around, she looks at nothing else but me.

'Our mother was not right in the head,' I try again, hoping to reach Ash somehow. 'What she did to you does not have to define you. I didn't let it define me!' I'll say anything at this stage to get Callie out of here. 'You and I. We're family. We're half brother and sister.' I nod at Callie. 'She's your niece! You don't have to do whatever that woman wants you to do.' I nod towards Clara. 'And trust me. Ava is a hundred shades of fucking mental. She loves no one but a monster who died years ago.'

'I love Ash now.'

'You love causing pain and misery.' I turn back to Ash. 'We have a new life here. We have freedom and safety for the first time in centuries. Don't destroy it after everything it took to get here.'

'I'm not going to destroy anything,' he says plainly, crouching down so he's eye level with me. It takes all I have not to spit in his face. 'The Arcane Realm will thrive, as will the witches within it. None so much as *my* Coven who have lived in hiding for so long. I will be their leader. I will create peace and order. I will get what I deserve and avenge those who were murdered all those years ago.'

'And I will be at his side,' Ava declares, thrusting out her chest and standing tall.

Ash leans in close. 'You, with your perfect family. Doted on by your people. Admired and celebrated for nothing more than being born lucky.'

'Lucky?' I whisper before bursting into laughter. 'Lucky?! Do you think anything about my life has been lucky? You have no idea the hell I have been through. And I will not stand by and let you take control over this realm. Not with your poisonous magic that destroys and kills the innocent.' I look at Ava. 'And not with her.'

'No. You won't stand by. Because you won't be here.' He stands and pulls out his scythe. I watch it closely, recalling my vision.

But he turns and goes to the altar, collecting the chalice.

'It's time for me to take my rightful place as the one and only Arcane.' He stands over one of the witches lying on the floor. 'With their death brings life to my dormant powers. Let's start with Elemental.' He kneels beside the man at his feet, who groans in terror, helpless and unable to move.

'Callie! Close your eyes, baby. Close them and keep them shut!' I tell her.

My sweet girl does as she's told.

Ash starts to speak archaic words as he cuts the man's throat and holds the chalice at his neck.

He walks away, leaving him to choke on his blood, and makes his way to the next one. All the while, Ava dances and claps her hands like a child.

Ash continues to mutter his words, casting his spell, and does the same to the next person. He slices deep and collects the blood as it spills furiously from their bodies.

And then the next, and the next.

I pull, and I pull at my ropes. I feel my bones strain and crunch. My skin bleeds as I struggle.

No matter what I do, I can't get free.

As the blood seeps from his victims, it trails in the dirt, moving with purpose. It forms a shape.

A seven-pointed star.

Just as it did in my vision.

He's killed five.

There is one more before it will be my turn to die.

He stands over Gabriel.

'The only witch left, except yourself, of course, Lilly, to wield Mental magic,' Ash says in a chilling calm, watching me closely as he rests the blade at Gabriel's throat.

Gabriel's eyes land on mine.

'Don't.' I pull against the ropes. 'Don't! PLEASE!'

Ash smirks, and he cuts.

I scream like a wild beast torn in two as Gabriel's blood spills down his front.

Ash collects his blood before dropping Gabriel carelessly back to the floor.

Gabriel looks at Callie.

My eyes land on our daughter, who still has her eyes scrunched closed.

I tried so hard to keep her safe. To protect her from harm and danger. To protect them all.

Ash stands beside me and wraps his fingers in my hair before tugging it tightly.

I watch the blood from the others continue to meld, forming that star around the Bloodstone and Callie.

With a blink, I look into Ash's eyes. Hot tears blur my vision as I meet his stare.

'The blood, all taken from those who wield one of the seven realms, mixed with the remains of the unborn unicorn, will awaken my dormant realms of power. It will bring life to the Arcane bloodline I inherited from my bitch of a mother, the power which refused to come forth because I was born without the bond of love. The bond between mother and child.' He looks at the bloody bowl his mother places at his feet. The one filled with pulverised flesh and bone from the stolen unicorn foetus. 'There's nothing more powerful. And harnessing it is something you will never forget until you die. Which for you, is in about ten seconds.'

'What about my daughter? Why is she here? You don't need her. Let her go!'

'I need an Arcane to keep on hand. Kept safe. Kept close. Kept so I can keep my access to the Arcane Realm alive forever. You see, dear sister. There is a special place, another realm if you like, where Dark Magic dwells. Just as the Arcane Realm gives magic to you and your kind, this realm feeds our magic. I hear it's quite the living hell. My lovely niece will be kept there, locked up nice and tight for the rest of time, so I can access her power whenever I want. It's the only downside to this type of magic. It's powerful, yes. More powerful than you could ever imagine. But it demands a sacrifice. It demands blood. So every time I perform this ritual, revitalising the magic you are all about to give me, I must make an offering. And Callie here will be the battery that charges the Dark Realm, boosting my Arcane gene into life.' He leans down and sneers the words. 'I don't need love to give me power. You and your daughter, along with all your weak and pathetic people, will give me all I fucking need.'

I look at Callie, still tied to that Bloodstone. Trapped. Doomed.

And I look at Gabriel, bleeding to death at my side.

A sharp sting erupts over my throat. Warm liquid gushes down my front.

Ash lets my head go. It lolls forwards and I watch the deep red of my blood pour down my chest. He rests the chalice close and captures some before collecting the bowl and walking away to the Bloodstone.

My blood pools around me. My life slowly ebbs further and further from my grasp. My ears ring. My vision starts to fade.

I blink.

I take a strained breath, and I whisper one final word.

'Callie...'

Chapter 20

The ground trembles. The roof starts to rain down chunks of stone as a deep rumble echoes all around us.

There's an explosion of red light that almost blinds me. I struggle to lift my head, but when I do, I see Ash, Ava and Clara being tossed through the air by streaks of red lightning, as well as the freaks standing around us in those dark robes.

The whole chamber shakes. The streaks shoot all over the place.

And then I realise that there's another sound.

A scream.

A furious, raging, brutal scream.

I look.

And see Callie, covered in those red streaks and sending them out in all directions, attacking the walls. The ceiling. Ash, Ava and Clara.

Callie's scream rebounds all around us, and with a final yell, the ropes tying her to the Bloodstone snap. She scrambles to her feet, pulls off her gag, and runs toward me.

She falls to her knees, looking at the wound around my throat in utter horror.

'Mummy...' she cries, turning to Gabriel. 'Daddy. What do I do? What do I do??'

'Take...' I choke on the blood filling up my airway. 'Off... my binding spell. Wrist.'

She reaches behind me and starts pulling at the binding spell at my wrist.

But she screams as she gets dragged away from me by an unseen force, clawing at the dirt as she fights against it. Clara is painfully getting back on her feet and has her hand outstretched as she summons my daughter towards her.

Ava cowers at the far side of the cave like the pathetic cretin she is. And the rest of this dark Coven are returning to their positions and sealing us inside.

The blood from the star completes and the Bloodstone starts to change colour. The once-clear pillar slowly turns dark. It moves like tar, oozing upwards and spilling out the top and dripping down the sides. When it hits the ground, it hisses and burns on contact.

I feel it. The magic inside is screaming at me like a demon. The air turns ice cold and becomes charged, like a battery on my tongue, but all over my body. It smells like death, rotten meat, and putrid blood.

My Sensativa feels its twisted nature. Its unnatural state. Its immense power.

Ash grabs Callie and closes his arms around her tiny body, lifting her up easily. He carries her, thrashing and screaming, towards the poisoned Bloodstone.

She's not screaming because she fears him. She's screaming for Gabriel and me, terrified that she is watching us die bloody before her very eyes.

'Hold still, you little shit!' Ash barks at her. 'Or I'll give you another slap.'

He drags her towards the stone, and again, she screws up her face and lets out a furious scream. Her body explodes in red lightning again. Ash roars in pain but refuses to let go, creating his own lightning to fend off hers. Sparks fly all over the place. The whole cavern trembles as more chunks get blown from the roof.

The star of blood starts to burn, like the tar substance still oozing from the bloodstone.

And I burn too. The blood left inside my body. The blood surrounding me.

I blink, watching as he drags my daughter closer and closer to the Bloodstone.

And when Callie's hand touches the tar, she screams. Her hand burns. The skin on her tiny fingers blister and blacken all at the same time.

And as she looks at me, her beautiful eyes full of undiluted terror, Callie fades into smoke and gets pulled into the Bloodstone.

The cavern no longer trembles with her power.

Callie, my daughter... is gone.

Chapter 21

A sh runs to the chalice and drinks the blood within it. He then eats a handful of the mixture in the bowl as he turns to face the blackened Bloodstone.

As he says his dark prayer to the Dark Realm he just sent my daughter to, the star of blood starts to glow.

And I feel myself flood with magic unlike anything I have ever felt before. A Dark Magic. A twisted and contorted power but fuck... it's so intense. So unyielding. It's a high like no other. My Sensativa senses power. It can take it and harness it. I am part of this spell. I am part of that darkness. And I am going to tear these fuckers to pieces.

I lift my head and heal the gaping wound on my neck. I burn the ropes around my wrist. I turn the binding spell to ash. It's nothing compared to this.

I stand and face Ash and watch as my hair turns black.

'Behind you!' Clara yells to Ash.

She reaches out her hand, daring to use her magic against me. I flex my fingers and twitch them. That's all. Just a twitch.

Her body bends and twists and snaps and breaks. Every bone. Over and over and over. Her eyeballs pop. Blood gushes from her ears, eyes, nose, and mouth. Her skin turns purple as blood erupts from her organs.

And I drop her to the floor without a care.

Ash looks at his crumpled-up mother and lets out a pained whine.

'Oh, look. I killed another one of your mummies. Whoops.'

I sweep my hand through the air and my fire springs to life at the feet of every one of his Coven members.

As they scream and try to escape the flames, Ash turns to face me. As he does, his eyes go black. His hair too, polluted by the unnatural magic. Fire erupts on his trembling fists. Lightning shoots from his body. The ground shakes and rocks lift from the floor.

He releases a warrior's cry and reaches out his hand, ready to try and tear me apart.

I hold him off easily as I tap into this darkness.

Ava screams as she charges toward me with a knife in her hand.

Before she can get close, she's sent flying through the air by a wall of fire.

Not my fire, though.

The black and white flames return to their creator, leaving her to stagger clumsily to her feet.

'T-Toby?' Ava stutters.

I turn to the cavern entrance and see all my people standing there.

Dad, Amara, Collins and Bias. Along with at least ten members of the Council.

Bias blinks at Ava. A look of disgust on every inch of his face.

'My Toby...' she whines, stumbling towards him. 'My beloved.'

Toby sends out another wave, sending her crashing hard into the rocks and leaving her to fall on the floor unconscious.

They all look at me, covered in copious amounts of blood. Tears silently streaming down my face and my eyes and hair as black as night.

'Where's Callie?' Dad demands. He sees those on the floor, bleeding and dying. He sees Gabriel. 'My god...'

Ash diverts his attack to them, sending vicious flames at them all.

Bias leaps in front and fends off his attack as Collins rushes to the aid of those still bleeding on the ground. To the youngest boy, who lies beside his grandmother's pale corpse.

She's gone, but the boy still blinks.

Ash attacks with his Telekinesis, trying to send them all back through the air.

Amara leaps in, making Ash slide back in the dirt a little.

I look at Gabriel on the floor, still bleeding.

Still alive!

I land on my knees at his side and rest my hand on his throat, sealing the wound shut and letting him breathe again. He gasps and groans as I help him to sit.

'Callie...' he manages to speak before trying to get to his feet and head to the Bloodstone. 'Callie!'

He's too weak to fight. Too weak to even stand.

I kiss him on the lips.

'Destroy this Coven,' I tell him. 'Don't let them leave here alive.'

I take a breath and summon my magic, sending myself to Ash's back and wrapping my arms around his waist.

I will not leave my daughter alone. Never. Wherever she is and whatever she is facing, I will be by her side protecting her.

And I will not leave this man here to destroy everything I sacrificed so much for.

So, I send us both to the Bloodstone. We touch its surface, and just as it did with Callie, it claims us too.

We turn to smoke and fade away.

Far. Far. Away.

Chapter 22

I thought I knew hell. I thought I knew pain and fear.

I knew nothing.

This realm... this realm is darkness beyond darkness. It's pain beyond pain. Horror beyond horror and evil beyond evil.

What I see. What I feel. What I hear and all I know turns to nothing in an instant.

The sky bleeds. The ground rots. The air burns and the sounds of monstrous screeching and howling are loud enough to make my ears rupture.

I'm quick to my feet and see Callie huddled in a ball with her arms over her head as she screams.

I run to her, tripping over vines of blood and bile that stretch over the endless landscape. I reach down and take her in my arms. She clings to me and I to her.

When I look back, I see Ash getting to his feet. His form is changing. The darkness already in him is being fed by the darkness that makes this place. He grins a monstrous grin as his form gets taller. His skin turns grey. His muscles grow as he throws back his head and lets out a victorious laugh.

'Bringing me here was a mistake, sister. It feeds my powers. It makes me a god!'

The vines start to slither and squirm towards us, entangling around my feet and climbing up my legs.

'You shall both stay here,' he says. 'This will be your home and you will keep my magic strong and unbeatable.'

In the distance, I hear a voice. A simple command bellowed with determination and absolute power.

A voice I know well.

And it orders Callie and I home.

Gabriel's Mental magic calls us back, piercing the barrier separating us.

I close my eyes and summon my magic.

And I follow his order to return to his side.

'Right fucking now!' he commands.

I land back in the cavern with my daughter in my arms. Gabriel runs towards us, his eyes still black, and wraps his arms around us both.

'You heard me,' he whispers. 'I knew you would.'

The cavern is quiet. Three of the missing witches have been healed, but two lie still and ghostly white in a pool of blood.

Six of the Dark Coven members are dead. Some burnt. Others with broken skulls. Four are on their knees with their hands tied behind their backs.

And ahead of me, gagged and restrained at Collins's feet, is Ava.

She weeps as she looks longingly at Bias, who refuses to meet her gaze.

'Ava...' I snarl. 'You're dead...'

The Bloodstone groans from behind us.

I turn and see a form in the thick tar that swirls inside it. Then, from deep within, long, thin and razor-sharp fingers start to push through, dripping with the black ooze.

'It's Ash,' I state in horror, knowing the monster he has become. 'He's coming.' I reach out my hand. 'He can't escape! We have to destroy the Bloodstone!'

The liquid hisses and bubbles and I watch his hand reach into this realm.

Into *my* realm.

I release my fire and send it at the stone. The monstrous hand winces but keeps pushing on.

'You heard her!' Amara bellows, running forwards and stretching out her hand. 'Destroy it! Everyone, now!'

She sends out a concentrated stream of her Telekinetic power.

Bias is next, sending more fire. Dad too. Gabriel faces it. His eyes blacken.

'Retreat,' he orders. 'Stand down. Stop pushing through.'

The hand withdraws, a raging roar resounding from within as it does.

But the damn thing won't break.

The others stand at our side and all throw their magic at it. The entire council, side by side with us.

Then Callie reaches out her hand. Her skin is still burnt and blackened from touching it.

'GO AWAY!' she screams.

We all get thrown back as the Bloodstone explodes in a blindingly white light of pure, untainted Arcane power. Shards of it fly in all directions. We all throw our hands over our heads to protect ourselves.

The cavern falls silent and still.

The Blood star dies.

The Dark Magic is gone. I no longer feel it and can no longer tap into it.

As we sit, I reach up and send a stream of fire to the ceiling, lighting the room back up so we can see what damage or death has been caused.

The others and the Council slowly sit, groaning and holding various injuries, but still helping each other and ensuring everyone is okay.

I look down and see Callie is still in my arms.

She's out cold. I give her a little shake and she grumbles in response.

'Is she okay?' Gabriel asks, rushing to my side and brushing her hair from her face.

I rest my hand on her forehead.

'She's asleep. Exhausted herself.' I lift my gaze to meet his and hold her red hair between our fingers. 'She's an Arcane.' A lump forms in my throat. 'She manifested because of fear and anger, Gabriel. This wasn't supposed to happen!'

'She'll be okay, Beautiful. We've got her.' He rests his hand on my cheek. 'You got her. Where did you go?' He looks at the crater where the Bloodstone once stood. 'You both disappeared for almost an hour.'

'An hour?' I ask. 'No. It was minutes.'

He shakes his head. 'I kept yelling and yelling. I even touched the Stone, hoping it would take me, but it didn't.' He shows me his raw hand, all blistered and charred like Callie's.

The same as my right shoulder where I touched it too.

'I heard you,' I tell him, leaning in and resting my forehead against his. 'We both did. You called us back.'

'I'm sorry to interrupt,' Dad says, kicking one of the Dark Coven members in the face when they try to stand. 'But what the hell happened here?' He looks at Clara's mangled corpse. 'Was she... Did she... W-what the fuck happened here?!'

'You have really awful taste in women, Dad. Truly.' I look at Gabriel. 'Let's get the hell out of here.'

Chapter 23

As Callie sleeps soundly on the sofa, I hold her hand. No matter how hard I try to fix it and heal those burns, they refuse to leave her body.

I tell them all what happened. I tell them who Ash truly was. I tell them what he and Clara did.

'Is he still alive?' asks Amara, taking the tea Connor offers. 'Ash?'

'I think so,' I reply. 'But he's trapped. Sealed away in that Dark place.' I lift my worried gaze to meet hers. 'He's powerful. He's an Arcane now. He unlocked all his powers, and they are powerful. That magic was... it was something else. But he's trapped over there.'

'Shame,' Gabriel mutters, gazing at Callie. 'I would very much like to repay him for all of this.'

'They said there were others like them. Other witches that practise Dark Magic. They said they had their own coven and had plans. More of The Stolen could be with them, or join them if offered the chance to return to the human world.' I look at them all. 'There could be more besides the ones we killed or caught.'

'Their leader is gone. As is their weapon,' Gabriel says. 'Without an Arcane, there is no way to access that place again. We will destroy what remains of the Bloodstones.

Turn them all to dust. And we will search this whole realm for any others who may have been in that coven.'

I stroke Callie's brand-new red hair.

'She's an Arcane now, and we must protect her and guide her at every turn.' I look again at her hand and I take in a shaky breath. 'I want to know of every single man born with access to Energy magic.'

'Why?' Amara asks.

'Because someone with that magic is going to kill Callie.'

'What?!' Gabriel says in a hush.

I show him her hand. 'Look familiar?' I ask, watching him closely as he looks at our girl's scarred hand.

'Shit...' he whispers, his fingers resting on the edge of his lip. 'But... it was you. We saw you in your vision.'

'We saw a woman who looked like me, with my hair. We saw an Arcane with a burnt hand die. And the man who kills her has lightning on his hand. Ash is gone. He's trapped. But there are witches who will still meddle with the Dark Magic. There aren't many. They admitted that themselves. But they are out there. And I want them all caught. And I want every man, woman and child with Energy magic listed and monitored. From now until the end of time. Because no one will hurt my child. Not again. Not ever again.'

I rest my hand on her head and delve into her mind. And I take away the memories of what happened tonight. I take away her memories of the death and blood and carnage. I eradicate the memories of the horrors she saw and felt in that other realm. I take it all.

Her dreams will remain just that. Dreams.

No nightmares. Not for her.

Never for her.

Chapter 24

*T*wo weeks later...

I walk hand in hand with Callie and Gabriel as we pass through the village. The witches all stop and smile warmly at their new Arcane. Callie blushes as they show her nothing but kindness and respect, bowing their heads at us both as we make our way towards the Council meeting.

Callie sits to the side, too busy with Finley and their toys to listen to us all talking.

I'm never letting her out of my sight again, that's for damned sure.

'The two remaining Bloodstones have been destroyed. I made sure of it,' I tell them all as they sit around the large, round table with me. 'They were utterly obliterated from the face of the earth. I don't see how Ash could leave that realm and return to ours.'

Gabriel takes my hand and addresses the council himself.

'My brothers and I...' Gabriel gestures to Bias and Collins. 'We discovered the location of the Dark Coven from one of the prisoners. We cleansed it.'

Killed them. Every single one.

'There are whispers of a few who escaped us,' he continues. 'But we will continue to look for any sign of Dark Magic and deal with it swiftly.'

'Speaking of the prisoners?' asks a council member, his eyes flicking between Bias and me. 'What of the girl?'

'Ava Sinclair succumbed to her injuries late last night,' I reply, feeling everyone in the room tense at the mention of her name. 'She was injured in the fight at the Bloodstone and refused healing. Her fate was her own, but she had proved useful before she left and provided us all the details we needed in order to find the Dark Coven.'

'That weasel was always quick to snap when put under pressure,' Gabriel mutters, still refusing to say her name.

'We need to be diligent, ladies and gents,' I declare, getting to my feet. They all follow suit. 'We know of two other realms besides ours that pose a considerable threat if they ever manage to seep into our home. The Human Realm and the Dark Realm. We must be on constant guard. Which reminds me, I visited The Stolen yesterday. They have taken up the offer of their own island. I will oversee their transportation myself. Many of them, however, did choose to join us. And their children have made a move to our village also.'

I feel Gabriel's eyes on me. I know he's watching me and biting his tongue.

What I am saying isn't a total lie.

They are relocating to an island. Just not by choice.

And we do have their children.

But again, it was hardly their decision.

I stepped into their camp and saw nothing had changed. They were all starving and dying in squalor. Two children were on death's doorstep before I healed them. And their porn-addicted leader tried, and spectacularly failed, to stab me.

I did not fail in breaking both his arms.

I warned them. Many times, I warned them.

No child will die through the stupidity, cruelness, or hatred of another for as long as I breathe.

I turn to Callie and hold out my hand. She scoops up her toys and runs to me, taking my hand in hers.

It's still scarred, but it causes her no pain.

None of our scars do.

And she recalls nothing. As far as she is aware, she woke up in bed with her magic. And she was thrilled, playing with her gifts and smashing way too many pots and plates in the process.

'Our village is growing. I would like you to send a team to another settlement fifteen miles east and start making plans for habitation. Clean, running water. Farms. Sanitation and comfort are key. They will need a council too. One to work with us as a team.' I pick Callie up in my arms.

They all bow as we turn and leave.

Me, Callie, Gabriel, Bias, Connor, Mama and Papa Quinn, Amara, Collins, Finley and Dad. We all leave together.

Back in the village, Callie runs ahead with Finley to play and chat with some more children up ahead.

To my left, Connor grins at the tiny dragon whose head is poking out from his jacket pocket, yipping with joy at him as he tickles his snout.

I think back to what he said to me at his camp that night when I asked why the baby dragon was alone in the rocks, left to die.

'I guess his mum abandoned or tossed him from the nest. Animals do that sometimes when a child isn't exactly how they want them to be. They leave them behind to die and move on to their next attempt at furthering their bloodline.'

That's precisely what happened to Ash. Born so innocent and then abandoned because he was not what she wanted. Locked up and left to die after knowing nothing but violence, torment and hatred at the hands of our mother.

Never again...

I take Gabriel's hand and stop.

'I have an errand to run,' I tell him, throwing my arms around his neck and standing on my tiptoes to kiss him. 'You good with Callie for a bit?'

'Stupid question,' he grins. 'Of course. But what errand?'

'Nothing major. No need to worry. I'll be home before you know it.'

He leans in and we share a kiss. One that gets interrupted by a happy squeal. We turn to see Callie jumping up and down as a tiny fire puppy stumbles around her feet.

'She's getting good and fast,' Gabriel admires a little nervously. 'I think we're going to have our hands full.'

'No,' I smile back. 'We're going to be absofuckinglutely perfect.'

I stand at the very top of the old shaft covered by an iron grate and smile before summoning my magic and sending myself below. I land with grace in the darkness and with a swish of my hand, I send my fire above, illuminating the small hidden place.

This cell, deep underground with no natural light and only the slightest fresh air from the hole hundreds of meters above.

There's a high-pitched scream and a rattle of chains. I laugh as Ava hurtles herself towards me and roll my eyes when the chain around her neck tugs her back and tosses her to the floor.

'Good afternoon, Ava Sinclair. And how are you feeling?' I ask, unwilling to even attempt to hide my smirk.

Her skin is bruised and grey. She's in a cream dress which is covered in filth and grime. And I can't tell if it's terror or rage that has her eyes so wide.

'Let me out of here, you fucking bitch!' she screeches, tugging at the chain frantically.

'You're not having fun?' I ask, pouting out my lower lip before chuckling. 'You sure had fun when I was chained up. How's that collar treating you?' I trail my finger across my own throat. 'You feel the binding spell I added to it for you? Nice, huh?'

'You can't keep me down here!' She looks around her in panic. 'There's no light. No fresh air. It's choking me. And the rats...' She looks in the corner where a few rat remains lie rotting.

'Got hungry, did we?' I jeer.

She coughs and shuffles from foot to foot.

'That tickle in your throat?' I gesture to my own. 'I used to get that a lot too. That's the mould and the damp. It will only get worse, I'm afraid.'

'If you want to kill me, just kill me.' She sniffles and snorts on her own sobs. 'Does Toby know I'm down here like this?'

'Toby is dead, Ava. He's long dead and he's never coming back.'

'I could bring him back,' she spits, suddenly finding some fire in her belly. 'One night with me and–'

'He didn't give a flying fuck about you then and he sure as shit wouldn't now, even if he did return. Which he won't. Bias is with someone else now. And he has his family and friends around him. He has us. And he is not into psycho-pathic whores who enjoy watching someone beat unborn children to death!'

Saying those words fills me with hate, and I twitch my fingers before I can stop myself. Her leg snaps, and Ava goes down in an agonised cry of pain, her leg sticking out at an unnatural angle.

'You are responsible for a lot of my misery and suffering, Ava Sinclair.'

'And you stole the only man I ever loved!' she wails in response. 'The way he looked at you... he should have looked at me like that!'

'And that justifies all you have done? A man, incapable of love, was obsessed with my magic. That's all. He tore me to pieces again and again. Manipulated and abused me. Beat me. Stood by as I was raped for years. Watched me cry myself to sleep because I was so hungry and scared. He scarred my body for pleasure.' I step closer, hot with hatred. 'He killed my unborn child, Ava. And you helped him do all those things. Your actions didn't make him love you. It just suited him. Amused him. But Toby Smith? He's dead. I killed him. Tobias killed him. He is never coming back.' My mouth twitches in a smirk. 'And neither are you. I am leaving here now,' I tell her. 'I'm returning home, where my husband sits with my daughter at a large table in my kitchen, smiling and laughing, surrounded by the rest of my family. By my Dad. The Quinns. Tobias. Collins and Amara. Lilah and Finley-'

She starts to laugh. Her twisted, criminally insane kinda laugh.

'You never asked me,' she says, drool spilling from her lips as she struggles to deal with the pain of her mangled leg. 'What my realm of power is.'

'Whatever it is, it's nothing compared to any one of mine.'

'It's Sight,' she spits. 'Oh and Lilly... the things I have seen. Do you want to know what I have seen? Do you want to know because if you kill me, you will never-'

My fingers twitch again and she wails as her jaw dislocates, leaving her mouth trapped open. Her wide eyes look at me in pure horror and pain as she wails.

'You know what I want more than anything? I want you to suffer, Ava Sinclair,' I tell her. 'I want you to be in so much pain, so afraid, so lost, and so desperate that you beg for the end. That you pray for it. I want your heart to break again and again until nothing of it is left. I want you to feel so doomed and trapped that the hopelessness will crush you from the inside out. I want you to suffer such grief that you can't breathe. That you won't want to.' I crouch before her as she continues to cry and drool. 'I can think of no hell worse than the life I have lived. So my punishment is exactly that. For you to live my life. To live through my memories. Every single one of them, over and over. And you will know true hell by the end.' I reach out and rest the tips of my fingers at her temple. My eyes blacken. 'You will be thrilled to know that my strength and stamina got quite the boost after I tapped into Ash and his Dark Magic. So this won't even give me a headache.'

She shakes her head, pleading with me to stop.

'You will live it all. Every second of my life. And you will feel it all. Every single bit. My Uncle's torture. Ryan's abuse. Toby's sadistic love. The Miller's Barn. Those years I spent in that cellar. Everything that happened at The Orchard. Everything that came after. Every single moment... I give to you.'

Her eyes roll back in her head as I send her all my worst memories. They fill up her head and swallow her whole. And whilst I am there, I take from her the visions she has seen.

A vision of Callie being stabbed by a man with lightning on his hands.

A vision of her falling to the floor and taking her last breath.

And a vision of darkness spreading throughout the village.

But also another vision. One that makes me smile. Because there is hope for us all. Ava just showed me what needs to happen for Callie to not only survive, but thrive, and become the most powerful, just, and beloved Arcane witch of all time.

I let Ava go and stand. Her eyes remain rolled back. Her jaw agape and her leg broken.

She whines and whimpers as she not just sees it all, but lives it as I did, feels it as I did.

I am content with the ending of this chapter in my life.

Ava Sinclair will be dead in a matter of days.

There is no food here. No water.

She will die suffering.

And that brings me peace.

'Goodbye, Ava Sinclair. You wanted my life so much... have it. Enjoy.'

With a whirl of wind, I fade from that dank hole, and return home.

Home...

Chapter 25

G abriel smirks as he slowly disappears beneath the duvet, trailing soft kisses down my body as he goes. As he reaches my belly and his hands clench under my ass, there's a light knock on the bedroom door and it slowly opens.

'Mummy?' Callie yawns, rubbing her eyes as she stands sleepily in the doorway.

Gabriel throws back the duvet and we both sit, covering ourselves.

'What's the matter, baby?' I ask, trying to keep my composure.

'I had a bad dream,' she grumbles.

'You did?' I soothe, reaching over and grabbing one of Gabriel's shirts to throw on. Dressed, I step out and head over to her, picking her up and letting her slump in my arms, already half falling back asleep. 'It was just a bad dream. It's over now.'

'And Finley is making too much noise. He keeps waking me up.'

'Is that so?'

She nods and yawns again.

'Well, you know Finley is at his house. He's not here.'

'He's shouting though. I can hear him.'

'How about you stay with us tonight, huh?'

'Ahhh, man...' Gabriel groans, looking sadly at his crotch.

I carry her to the bed and settle her in, tucking her down tightly and kissing her head as she already starts to return to sleep.

'Don't worry, husband. We always have tomorrow.'

'I'll be holding you to that.'

'I'll be holding something alright,' I smirk.

There's a loud bang on the front door.

'What now?' Gabriel groans.

'I'll go see.'

'I'll go.'

'You stay with Callie. It's Amara.'

'How do you know that?'

'I can sense her magic. Calm down. I'll be right back.'

I throw on a dressing gown and head downstairs.

When I reach the front door, I open it up.

Amara stands there looking as pale as I've ever seen her.

'Hey. What's the matter?'

'We need your help. Right now, we need your help.' She takes my hand and starts pulling me out of the house.

'What's happened?' I ask, trying to get her to calm down and stop.

'It's difficult to explain, but I really need you to come.'

'Is everything okay?' Gabriel asks as he descends the stairs, pulling on a shirt. He sees Amara's state and rushes closer. 'What's the matter?'

'I erm...' She looks at me pleadingly. 'I had a bad nightmare. I'm feeling a bit spooked. Lilly said she'll have a hot drink with me back at mine.' She forces a smile at Gabriel, hopefully reassuring him that all is well. 'I'll have her back to you in a bit. I promise.'

He glances at me, narrowing his eyes a little.

'I'll be back in a while,' I tell him. 'Everything is fine.' I have no idea what's going on, but Amara obviously doesn't want him to know about it.

'Well... okay. Be safe,' he says. 'If you need anything, I'm right here.'

Amara takes my hand and drags me out into the night, almost running down the path leading back to her cottage.

As soon as we enter her house, she seals the door shut and slumps her back against it. She just stares at me with tears streaming one after the other down her cheek.

'What's happened?' I ask, taking her hand in mine. 'Honey, please, you're scaring me.'

She takes a deep breath.

'Finley was asleep in bed,' she says, her words straining. 'I went to check on him and...'

My stomach drops.

'I can fix him if he's hurt. Take me to him.' I turn to run up the stairs. She tightens her grip on my hand and pulls me back

'He's healthy. He's... he's okay.'

'Then what is it?'

'He's... he's erm...' She clears her throat. 'He's manifested his magic,' she tells me. 'In his sleep.'

'But that's good, right?' I ask.

Her lip trembles and she shakes her head before walking down the hall and up the stairs.

She stops outside his bedroom door and opens it slowly.

Inside, Finley slumbers peacefully. At the end of his bed, Collins sits with his head in his hands. He looks up as the door creaks and gets to his feet quickly.

He looks just as devastated as his wife.

All seems well, except for the toys gently hovering in the corner of the room a few inches from the floor. They move as if they're being played with. Finley must be dreaming about playing with them.

'He's manifested your Telekinesis, Amara,' I whisper, looking and feeling completely lost at their reaction. 'Why are you so freaked out?'

'He has.' She swallows painfully. 'But that's not all he's manifested.'

As she looks into my eyes, I hear a slight crackle. Her gaze falls to the floor as mine slowly goes to her son.

'What the...' I step a little closer, bewildered at what I'm seeing.

On his hands, blue lightning sparks between his fingers. I stop at his bedside and stare at it, watching as it slowly snakes along his little fingers.

'How... I don't understand. This shouldn't be possible.' I look between Amara, who chews her lower lip, and Collins, who watches her with a pained expression.

'How does he have that power?' I ask them both. 'Children inherit their realm from their parents.'

'I hoped I was wrong. I pleaded with the universe not to let it happen.' Amara's lip trembles.

'You remember when we were separated after you were branded?' Collins says quietly. 'Grayson sent us away to Scotland and used us as leverage against you.'

All I can do is nod very slowly as my insides become lead. I think I know where this is going.

'Well...' Amara whimpers. 'He used Collins and me as leverage against each other too. One night, we tried to send you a message with a plan for our escape. We were caught. As punishment... Grayson... he... he erm...'

'He hurt Amara,' Collins says in barely a whisper. 'He hurt her to punish me.'

'We both chose to risk it,' Amara insists, stepping inside with us and going to Collins. 'What happened was not your fault. It was his fault. His cruelty.'

Collins pulls her into his chest, encasing her in his arms and holding her tight.

'I'm sorry. I'm so fucking sorry.' It's all I can think to say as I watch the two.

We both look at the lightning still sparking on her son's fingers.

'Lilly, he has the same power as the person you saw in your vision.'

'Don't be ridiculous,' I snap at Amara, perhaps a little too harshly considering the raw admission she's just made. 'There is no way that he would ever hurt Callie. He loves her to pieces. He's good. Hundreds of witches have that realm of power and there are hundreds yet to be born who will too.'

'I just...' Amara looks over at Finley with such love. 'I never want him to know who his biological father is, Lilly. Collins is his dad. He will always be his dad. I never want him to know what that monster did to me. To you. To us all. I never want him to think he is anything like that man. I know what my father did to my mother and my little sister, and I loathe that I have his blood in my veins. It disgusts me. I don't want Finley to ever feel that he has anything to fear from who he is.' She faces me. They both do. 'Can you help us?'

'Help you how?'

'Can you hide that he has that realm of power?' Collins asks. 'You took Callie's memories of what happened. You took the knowledge of the Brand from the minds of The Stolen. Can you do that here? Hide it so deep, it can never be found?'

'I...' I take another look at Finley, who smiles in his sleep, the two dolls hovering in the air dancing with each other. 'I don't think that's a good idea.'

'Grayson's name is dirt here, Lilly. He is beyond hated. If people learn that his son is here, they might come for him. No good will come from anyone learning the truth about this. Please!' Collins presses his hands together as if in prayer. 'He has Telekinesis. He won't be without magic!' He gestures to the toys in the corner. 'Only pain will come from him knowing about Grayson. Please?'

I look at them in turn. Each one is as desperate as the other to make this disappear.

I think of all the damage that has been done to those who know the truth about where they come from. Ash was obsessed with becoming a Hooper Arcane. So obsessed that it drove him mad. His hatred for our mother spilled out as hatred at the world. She hurt him. He wanted to hurt everyone.

I think of the fear I have of following in her footsteps too. I said it to Dad only a few weeks ago, how I dread hurting Callie as my mother hurt me.

And yes. I saw the very same lightning on the hand of the man who will attack my daughter.

I nod. And I sit by his bedside. I rest my hands on Finley's head and I close my eyes, channelling my powers into his very core.

And I bury deep the power he has manifested tonight. I bury it deep, and I lock it away.

And I pray that this is the right thing to do.

Chapter 26

A fter...

I look around the room and can't help but smile. Bias and Connor fuss over the baby dragon rolling around in Connor's palm.

Dad is playing marbles with Callie and laughing as she cheats with her new Telekinetic magic.

Amara and Collins sit with their two children, toasting marshmallows over the fire in the fireplace.

Mama and Papa Quinn are in a deep conversation, discussing the possible properties of swamp moss mixed with dragon wee.

And I'm sat between Gabriel's legs, his arms wrapped around my middle and his chin settled on my shoulder. His warm breath lands on my skin and his scent surrounds me completely.

It's perfection. Every single bit of it.

And God help anyone who dares try and ruin a single second of it.

This realm is protected. This realm belongs to us, and no one will take it away.

Absofuckinglutely no one.

Beyond The Veil
Coming soon!

My name is Callie Kendryk.

I am an Arcane Witch.

My parents told me stories of how we escaped the human world and found safety and freedom in this realm.

I know my job is to protect it and all those who live here in peace.

And nothing makes me happier than doing precisely that.

But in the darkness of my dreams, I hear whispers. A threat from a place of darkness.

And a promise to make us all pay.

My mother warned me to be ready for a man with blue lighting on his hands with a plan to destroy everything. She made me promise to keep my friends and family close. To trust my instincts and always fight for what is right.

When I awake on my eighteenth birthday, I find a journal full of spells and warnings at the foot of my bed.

And in my parent's bedroom, I find blood.

Thank you

Thank you for reading The Last Witch 3.5
I hope that you enjoyed it.

Please take a moment to leave the book a rating or review.

Amazon
https://mybook.to/beyond-a-novella

Goodreads

Please feel free to follow me:

Facebook: @HelloMJLawrie

Instagram: m.j.lawrie_author

TikTok: MJ Lawrie_Author

Sign up to my newsletter here:
www.mjlawrie.com

Also by M. J. Lawrie

THE STOLEN FAE SERIES

Monster. Liar. Thief. Killer.
I've been called it all and so much worse. And they're
not wrong.

I've been running my whole life. Hiding from the monsters who haunt my dreams and who will tear me apart again and again if they ever find me. I live off whatever I can steal, trapped inside a fae prison city filled with pollution, sin and poverty. Humans have captured the Fae.
We belong to them now.
Cyrus, the egotistical and frustratingly gorgeous leader of the fae under-city, can't seem to decide whether he wants to kill me or claim me for his own dark and delicious desires.
And Reid, a dangerous and hypnotically beautiful human Authority Agent whose sole purpose should be to keep me in the dirt, has decided to keep me as his own personal Pet instead.
But when dark, demonic creatures start attacking, killing human and Fae alike, alliances must be made, especially when the monsters seem to be determined to find and slaughter me.

A dormant war is awakening, and the part I must play in it is only just becoming clear.
Do I stand and fight? Or do I strike the match and watch them all burn?

Available now on Amazon:

https://mybook.to/liesofthefae

THE VERITY DUOLOGY

Their Death. Our Glory!

The Lottery is the chance of a lifetime. The one and only hope a girl has to escape certain death as a sacrificial soldier,

fighting the bloodthirsty, flesh-tearing monsters that roam freely beyond "The Wall".

Put in your name, and if chosen, become wife to the powerful and gorgeous leader of the last of humanity.

Lord Noah Sands. A supposed living god amongst the last of humankind.

For Scarlett, winning The Lottery is a fate worse than death.

But Lord Noah Sands has only ever had eyes for Scarlett, and when he threatens the man she truly loves, Scarlett must make an impossible choice.

Available now on Amazon:

https://mybook.to/theverityone

Printed in Great Britain
by Amazon

35810211R00104